Flash

The Storm Dragons' Mate
Book 4

M. Sinclair

Lost & Bound Publishing

Flash: *The Storm Dragons' Mate 4*

Editorial Team:

Refined Voice Editing & Proofreading

 Formatted with Vellum

The Union of Love & Madness

Description

Clanguard has started a war—and I will do anything *to stop it.*

Eight years ago, Linan Clanguard successfully staged the attack and slaughter of my family's clan. I will not let it happen again. The proof of his betrayal lies in my parents' imprisonment—because after all of these years, the truth has been revealed. My parents are alive, and I just have to find a way to free them.

Unfortunately, my mates and I are struggling to locate my parents, let alone free them. But with the help of Rachel and her mates, as well as some witches from Carmina...we may just be able to pull it off before the clock ticks down to the start of sense-less bloodshed.

No matter what happens, one thing is clear—

Trabea, my mates, and myself will never be the same again.

Flash is book 4 in the **Storm Dragons' Mate series** that features a slightly naive but sassy MFC, possessive dragon alphas, and a secret that will change everything. This is not a high school academy book, and the contents are intended for mature audiences, with characters who are all 18+. This book includes violence and mature sexual content.

Author Note:

Flash is set in the shared universe of Dark Imaginarium Academy. All series can be read independently, but characters have crossovers and it is highly encouraged to read all within the universe to understand the world in its entirety.

Series within the Universe:

Phases of the Moon by M. Sinclair

The Creatures We Crave by R.L. Caulder

The Storm Dragons' Mate by M. Sinclair

Blood Oath by R.L. Caulder

Character Glossary

Blitz Clan

- Leopold Bronzeheart - Clan Leader
- Celine Bronzeheart - Clan Leader
- Gage Bronzeheart - Clan Leader Heir

Flicker Clan

- Arnold Silvershade - Clan Leader
- Marilyn Silvershade - Clan Leader
- Jagger Silvershade - Clan Leader Heir

Surge Clan

- Trek Firespell - Clan Leader
- Darla Firespell - Clan Leader

- Breaker Firespell - Clan Leader Heir

Flash Clan

- Jericho Blackforge - Clan Leader
- Ashley Blackforge - Clan Leader
- Bexley Blackforge - Clan Leader Heir
- Rebecca - Clan Leader Advisor

Clanguard Pack

- Linan Clanguard - Alpha
- Carol Clanguard - Alpha's Mate
- Thomas Clanguard
- Fletcher Clanguard - Future Alpha
- Olivia Clanguard

Avian Shifters

- Chanelle Spencer - Alpha
- Kelvin Spencer - Alpha's Mate

Water Shifters

- Ciaran Bowman - Alpha
- Angelica - Alpha's Mate

Bear Shifters

- William - Alpha

Feline Shifters

- Alpha Fangce - Alpha
- Treya Fangce - Alpha Fangce's Sister

Prey Community

- Annika - Council Leader

Rogue Lands

- Dyer - Rogue Land Leader
- Aurora

Chapter 1

Bexley Blackforge

I would do *anything* to ensure the people I loved came out of this situation alive.

The thought reminded me of what was truly important—not the war right outside our door, nor the violent demand for revenge that ravaged through my brain—no, there would be time for that later. Instead, all that mattered in this moment were the individuals I loved, the ones I cared about protecting, many of whom were currently gathered around me. All of our eyes were on the approaching army outside, and the tower-like room we'd sheltered in was covered in broken glass from the blasted-in windows.

I couldn't—I wouldn't—let my emotions override what I needed to figure out. How did we get out of this situation without a complete slaughter?

The army approaching may have been the enemy, but that didn't mean they all deserved death. Especially if they were being forced to fight. It was a concept that cooled my anger as I imagined how each and every one of the individuals approaching had families to return home to. There had to be a way to solve this without absolute carnage.

"Someone leaked the meeting." Annika's accusation rang out sharply. My gaze moved toward the delicately built woman, her short dark hair smoothed away from her elegant features. Her face was twisted into a fierce expression, filled with fiery anger that made her look absolutely lethal. It probably didn't help that she looked like she'd just come from a battlefield, her dress covered in debris from the explosion.

As one of the council leaders for the prey community, Annika had a way of talking that spoke to experience and leadership, despite her being considered 'less dominant' than many other shifter species.

Or *that* was what we were taught—I was finding that it was far more complex than that.

"Walker, my beta." Fletcher concluded, his jaw tight with anger as he ran his hand through his dark reddish hair in agitation. "I didn't tell him about the meeting or what we were doing, but he was probably notified when the three of us left campus. If he's working with my father, I'm sure he pieced it together."

"He's a piece of shit, but he's not stupid," Professor Clanguard agreed, as Rachel, who was positioned between the two of them, nodded in agreement. "And even if Walker hadn't put it together, our father would have—especially considering our lack of communication with him."

Linan Clanguard. The mere mention of his existence caused hate to grow even heavier in my heart. The man was central to this senseless violence. The cause of our problems from start to finish, it seemed.

The man who attacked and killed the Flash clan.

The man who kidnapped my parents and held them prisoner for over eight years now.

The absolute monster who'd clearly made it his goal to finish what he'd started long ago.

"We should've taken care of our father before now," Fletcher admitted.

"You were mere children, you can hardly be blamed," Celine Bronzeheart said, her eyes filled with sympathy for the wolf shifters.

"It doesn't matter now," William, the alpha of the bear shifters, said—his harsh tone causing me to stiffen slightly. I may not have been as close to Fletcher and Professor Clanguard as I was to Rachel, but I still didn't like how he was talking to two individuals I considered my friends. "The past is inconsequential. We need to focus on the army of wolf shifters approaching the estate. We don't have many defenses up, and if we let them move in any closer it could be game over. We don't have the numbers to combat them properly right now."

He was right. We needed to figure out a plan—and quick—or else they would be at our door in no time. A problem made even more dire since the majority of the leaders had come to the Silvershade estate for this meeting.

"It's not a problem of numbers," Trek Firespell said. His look of utmost confidence baffled me, considering the situation at hand.

"How is it not a problem of numbers?" I asked, feeling all eyes turn to me at once.

The Bronzehearts, Silvershades, and Firespells were only the ones whose gazes I found a tad comfortable—at least compared to the council leaders of the city communities of the prey, aquatic, avian, feline, and bear shifters. It felt almost suffocating, the amount of power in the room, and I found myself glad that Rachel was part of the crowd and that my mates stood behind me in a wall of security and familiarity.

"Because we could slaughter all of them—easily,"

he responded bluntly. Breaker let out a low rumble at the way I recoiled at his father's words.

"Trek," Mrs. Firespell warned.

"She should know and understand that they aren't a real threat. All it would take is an electrical storm—"

"They are if we don't want to kill them," Leopold Bronzeheart interrupted.

"And we don't," I said in a hard tone. "They may not even want to fight. Have we considered that Linan may be forcing them? Have we considered that they have families back in the pack lands?"

The room went silent. I may have sounded naive, but much like the hierarchy of society that was established with shifters—I wasn't going to buy into it. This didn't have to end in bloodshed.

"That is the game of war." Marilyn Silvershade offered me a heartbreaking look. I could see that Mr. Silvershade was in deep thought, but he didn't offer his opinion, making me think he agreed with what she was implying—that it was unavoidable.

"Well I'm not playing. Besides, that tactic may work to our advantage in the moment, but will an outright slaughter help us in the long run? Will losing a massive part of the Trabea population make anything truly better?" Jagger wrapped an arm around me in silent support, Gage intertwining the fingers of my left hand with his. "Besides...I know what Linan really wants, and it's not war."

"And what's that?" Alpha Fangce asked. As a feline shifter, there was something intently predatorial to the way he tilted his head with curiosity, seemingly unruffled by this entire situation. I had no idea where his sister Treya had gone. I'd been surprised he'd brought her to begin with, and I couldn't help but worry she was downstairs in the midst of chaos.

"Me."

The room grew tight with tension, but there was a lack of true surprise. While I didn't think any of them had known Linan's true motives, it didn't seem to surprise them that there were possibly alternative ones. I drew in a deep breath, knowing I needed to explain this as simply and as concisely as I could.

Already I could hear the shouts and the preparations for battle downstairs as security around the estate prepared to defend it. Putting aside the security the other alphas had brought, the dragon clans had what were essentially military units that guarded their properties, so I had a small window of time to explain before the Clanguard pack was at our door.

The vision of their heavy artillery and at least a hundred of them marching under a flag with a wolf sigil painted in black and red flashed before my eyes.

"Explain," Alpha Spencer encouraged. Her

mate, Kelvin, stood staring down onto the battlefield, rolling back his shoulders as if preparing to shift—or sprout wings. I could almost feel everyone keying themselves up for battle.

"Okay, so." I nibbled my lip as Gage gave my hand a reassuring squeeze. "I'm going to just dive into this because I don't know where else to start."

"Take your time, everyone is willing to listen," Breaker assured me. I looked up into his mismatched gaze and steadied myself before returning my attention to the rest of the crowd.

"Right." I nodded before starting. "I'm not sure if many of you remember, but when my parents ruled over the Flash clan, they had several prophetesses who advised them on topics ranging from agriculture, upcoming events, even the prediction of storms—"

"As well as some decisions regarding conflicts," Celine interjected. "They were extremely helpful."

I offered her a thankful smile before continuing. "When I was young, a prophecy was presented to my parents that I only recently remembered. I was even able to confirm it, written down in a text about all the prophecies our clan had been given. It was about a female storm dragon uniting all four storm dragon lines."

I paused, waiting for the backlash but finding

only curiosity in most of their gazes. "Specifically, it read: *When the time comes that four lines are united by one heir who threatens everything created in the darkness, the territory will be made anew, reborn in the ashes of the cursed pack.*"

My gaze moved to the floor in thought as I admitted, "I'm sure that knowing about the prophecy doesn't help any suspicion you have toward us, but I know that it was one of the driving forces that instigated this entire situation with Clanguard. My mom tried to protect the women in his pack, including his wife—"

"Who he no doubt abuses to this day," Professor Clanguard—Thomas—hissed. "He hasn't allowed either of us to lay eyes on her since I left for the academy." My chest squeezed in pain at the thought of the suffering she was potentially undergoing—at the vision of the bruised woman in my memory that had come to my mom for help.

"When Linan heard the prophecy, he hoped to capture me to ensure that I would instead be mated to his son. To produce a line of storm dragons under his control." My face pinched with disgust, the tension in the room heightening. I wanted to turn to my mates for comfort, but I knew I couldn't—not yet.

"So he attacked and slaughtered his way through the Flash clan to find me. One of my mother's advisors helped me escape, though, and sealed my memories. He wasn't able to find me, but by then it was too late. He had killed nearly everyone. Now Linan is on the same mission as before—to capture me—and he's willing to sacrifice his own pack members and participate in the same amount of bloodshed as before." Grief at the lives lost clogged my throat as I tried to not overanalyze the reactions in the room.

"You poor girl." Alpha Spencer appeared before me, gently touching my shoulder. "This is not your fault, Bexley. Your clan's death, your parents' deaths, were Linan's doing. And *only* his."

Nodding, I offered her a small gratitude-filled glance as she stepped back. Deciding it was a better time than ever to reveal what I knew would be the hardest element to believe, I continued. "My parents are possibly still alive, held captive by Clanguard. Have been since that night."

Absolute silence.

"Holy shit." Alpha Bowman of the water shifters looked at me with unmasked shock, his brows raised impossibly high. "He was able to capture both of them and keep them locked up for—"

"Eight years," Celine Bronzeheart confirmed. Her eyes flashed with a dangerous anger as her lips pursed, clearly wanting to say more but choosing to restrain herself.

"How do you know?" Annika demanded.

"Our source is reliable. She'll be here soon—she was my mother's right hand," I explained. I knew Rebecca would be here in no time, but I desperately wished she was here now to support and lend credence to what I was saying.

"If he's taken another leader of the territory hostage, then this involves all of us—that is cause for war." William's voice was hard, his mind clearly made up.

"This attack is only the start; a warning of what's to come," Fletcher explained, his gaze moving out the window. "He hasn't sent all of his forces—not even half of them. My father isn't even out there. He *wants* you to decimate them so that his other men rise to the challenge to avenge those that die. My father has always been of the mindset that it's okay to sacrifice his own people for long-term gain."

"The storm dragon clans won't stand for this," Mrs. Firespell said sharply, her chin tilted up. "His time as a leader is over. His time ruling the city is over. The city has always been a place ruled by multiple factions, and unless I'm mistaken, that has been slowly changing over the past decade."

"It has, possibly longer than that. There's only so much we can do to fight back when often it's a game of numbers—when they make the smallest advances into our territories day by day. We've watched entire blocks of the city being taken over by the Clanguard pack, seemingly overnight." Alpha Fangce agreed. His eyes filled with heavy emotion, making it clear that the situation within the city was worse than we knew.

"We need to free your parents," Jagger said, his lips brushing the top of my head. "Right now he views their existence as a source of power for himself —a trump card. If we free them, he'll not only be weaker, but it'll show everyone what drastic steps he took to achieve power."

"Without them, Clanguard may hesitate to wage a full-scale war," Annika added. "Although, there are already so many of us...I would have to assume he's considered that and chosen to make this decision nonetheless."

"Unfortunately, his numbers rival even our clans', and it's possible that he may even be counting on us to hesitate, to not fully commit to slaughtering his people," Leopold pointed out. Considering I'd made it clear in that meeting that I wasn't a fan of violence or the shifter hierarchy, it was possible Mr. Bronzeheart was right about that—that Linan was counting on my ideals to stand in the way of Mr. Firespell's solution to ending this.

"My father always expects violence, so he probably isn't counting on that," Fletcher disagreed. "He may consider that it will make you hesitate for a moment, but he's still betting on your reaction to his attack. Without it he has no gasoline to throw on the flames of war growing within the pack."

"If this is a warning and he wants us to kill the army that's attacking, what do we do?" Kelvin asked, not turning from the window he'd been staring out of. The battle had started in earnest, our security defenses starting to clash with a group of wolf shifters who'd shifted and sprinted ahead to the front lines, the rest of the army only a mile or so out. Cries of pain and anger, paired with gunshots, filled the air.

"We let them capture the estate. Our security will take enough of them out so we can safely move our base of operations to one of the other territories," Jagger's dad said. "Linan will view it as a win. Some deaths are unavoidable in this." His gaze moved to mine, but I refused to nod in agreement, so he continued, "But we'll be in a better position to find out where their forces are building and what direction they'll come from. We have more than enough people here to ensure that we'll still have eyes on the property, to know his next move."

"Are you sure about that?" I asked, looking at Mrs. Silvershade. "You love your home." I knew she had put years of work into it, and if they took it over, who knew what would happen to it.

"Homes can be rebuilt, but lives cannot," she said softly as she walked over and gently squeezed my arm, my mates shifting slightly to accommodate. "More importantly, though, we need to get you out of here. This is a targeted effort—which means, Bexley, that you need to disappear until we can figure out how to release your parents."

"I won't hide from this," I warned. I was someone who normally agreed with the general plan, especially the plans of those who had more experience, but I wouldn't hide like last time. I wouldn't let history repeat itself.

"We're in more danger with you here," Annika said bluntly. "Like you said—he wants you."

I couldn't argue that.

"Plus, if you need to release your parents it would make sense if we"—Fletcher motioned toward Thomas and Rachel—"came with you. We have a much better idea of where they could be and how to infiltrate the pack lands."

Mr. Bronzeheart stepped forward. "Then it's decided. The seven of you will leave and focus on releasing Bexley's parents, and everyone else here will move locations. We need more time to plan, and if he knows you aren't here, he'll hesitate to make his next attack—he won't want to make a move until he knows his goal is within range. The current numbers can be handled by making a small example instead of a full battle—but any more and it could require more violence."

I knew it was the right move, though I hated the idea of leaving. Instead, I tried to keep the most important thing in mind: keeping as many people alive as possible. Even if it meant putting aside my need for vengeance and to stop Linan for good.

"Alright," I agreed quietly before looking at my mates. "Let's do this."

Chapter 2

Bexley Blackforge

"Everything will be fine, I promise," Celine assured me as Mrs. Firespell and Mrs. Silvershade stood nearby with their mates and Mr. Bronzeheart, everyone having already bid goodbye to us.

Following the meeting, I'd changed into dark leggings and a hoodie, our bags being packed quickly by staff as the sound of battle rang loudly outside. Night had fallen completely around the estate, so the tunnel we were in was dark, the faintest light at the end from a set of flickering torches marking our way out of the grounds.

"I know," I whispered, hating that her eyes were glossy. While she may have been reassuring me, I knew that her words were more for herself than anything. "I'm worried about all of you. I'm worried you won't make it to the other estate without problems."

"Oh, we'll be fine." She waved me off and looked toward my mates, who were standing nearby. "Boys, you better protect her."

"With our lives," Gage promised his mom.

"Plus, they have me!" Rachel squeaked from nearby. I loved that even though she was obviously nervous around so many dragons, she was trying to comfort Celine. I was glad she was coming with us, not only because it meant spending more time with my friend, but it also meant I could ensure she stayed safe. Of course I trusted that her mates could do that...but it still made me feel better.

"We should head out." Celine stepped back and nodded as Breaker approached, my gaze moving to my massive mate. He stood above everyone else nearby, which was saying something considering all the male shifters around. His muscular build, much like my other mates', was covered in dark clothing, and as I leaned into his side, I found myself wondering not for the first time how we physically fit together so perfectly.

I mean, seriously—perfectly. My body still remembered the sensation.

As if knowing where my thoughts went, his mismatched gaze—one eye completely black and the other gold—moved over my expression with heat, the gold seeming to melt while the black sparked dangerously, causing my heart to beat double-time.

Tonight Breaker's blonde hair was pulled away from his face, and the shadows of the cave partly hid the scar on his face. My fingers twitched, wanting to trace it. Even at this moment the man looked like a warrior, and I had to fight the urge to go up on my toes to get a kiss from him. I knew if he started touching me, I would be far too distracted to remember that we needed to get out of this estate as fast as we possibly could.

Luckily, Celine spoke up, reminding me of my audience. "Of course, of course. Keep your phones on you; we'll contact you once we've moved."

"Got it." Gage offered a sharp nod before exchanging a look with his dad. I offered all of them one last wave before we turned to follow Rachel and her mates out.

Breaker jogged ahead to walk alongside Thomas, something clearly having occurred to him. Gage and Jagger bookended me protectively, and while I always felt petite around my mates, I felt even more so now. The tension and lethal energy rolled off of them in a way that called to a base instinct of mine, even if I hated the reason the tension was there in the first place.

"I can feel how worried you are for them." Jagger plucked my right hand, brushing his lips against it. My mate's hair was pushed back from his face, the silver darkened to a charcoal in the shadows. Streaks of black broke it up, stark against his icy complexion, and his clear blue eyes, which were warm with concern and love. My gaze moved across his face, trying to gauge how he felt about this entire situation, before I examined the rune on his jaw. Suddenly, I found myself asking a question that had ping-ponged around in my brain for quite some time but I had continued to forget to ask.

"The rune on your jawline, what is that?"

Jagger's lips pressed into an immediate smile. Gage was looking through his phone and sending off messages, but he chuckled at my question, making me that much more curious.

"My mom's elemental specialty is ice. We have a language that developed centuries ago between ice dragons that was used primarily for text keeping. This is a rune from it. It's for the letter *B*."

My eyes widened. "Oh. *B* for..."

"Bexley, my little treasure—but I think you knew that," he mused, kissing my hand once more.

"I love that," I whispered as he gently pulled me to a stop. Gage kept walking, and I couldn't help but be thankful that my mates were so good at stuff like this. Somehow they knew instinctively when each of them needed a moment alone with me. It really felt like it was that simple. The bond may have helped, but I had a feeling a lot of it was because of their years of friendship.

Jagger cupped my jaw. "And I love you, Bex. You know that, right? You have to know how much I love you."

My heart squeezed as my eyes pricked with a rush of emotion that seemed to lodge itself in my chest, growing until it was painfully large. It was like a flood gate of love and affection poured out at once, and I fell into Jagger, kissing him hard on the lips as he swept me up against his frame.

Pulling back for only a second, I spoke in an intimate tone, only a mere inch between us. "Yes, I know. And I love you. So incredibly much."

Meeting his lips again, I poured every ounce of that intense passion I felt for him into our kiss and found myself turning into putty in his hands. I shivered at the way his tongue slid across my lips, and I only came back to earth when the clearing of a throat made me realize Gage was waiting for us.

The others had already made it to the end of the tunnel, their shadowy shapes making me wonder if I may have been distracted for a bit longer than I'd thought.

"Oops."

Gage's emerald eyes flashed with bronze as he shook his head in amusement. Jagger released his hold on me, admittedly a bit begrudgingly, and we continued walking forward, meeting up with my other mate, my face flushing at the way he stared at me. Despite having been in the arms of my other mate, I could see the heat and hunger written on his face, and it had me wanting...well, a lot of different things.

But mainly Jagger and Gage both with me...or maybe all three of them.

Pushing those distracting thoughts from my head, I took Gage's hand as Jagger stood on my other side. Going up on my toes, I pushed Gage's hood back with one hand, the reddish undertone of his dark hair and the gold to his complexion seeming to almost glow like it was lit from within. I could hear the others' voices ahead, and I found myself moving a bit faster now, my dragon urging me forward, wanting to get to a safe location as quickly as possible.

Not because I was worried about myself, but because I was worried about my mates—and I knew they probably felt the exact same way about me.

"Hey, Gage?" Jagger's story about his rune had me thinking. "What's Celine's element?"

"Fire—like your mom," he answered.

"And what about Breaker's mom?"

"Earth."

"Interesting," I murmured. "I feel like I need to know more about dragons, especially now that I remember I am one—it's sort of embarrassing. I mean...I feel like I've barely met any dragons to begin with."

"That's been purposeful," Gage admitted. "We didn't know how the memory spell would react to meeting other dragons, especially if they said something triggering. We also didn't trust their reaction to you. Luckily there aren't any that are academy-aged yet, so that made it easier. But if Linan is truly starting a war, I have a feeling you'll be meeting a lot of dragons very soon. The population isn't huge, but there are a fair amount."

I couldn't lie, the idea of meeting other dragons was appealing. As we caught up with the rest of the group at the end of the tunnel, I stood with Rachel just outside the door, the heavy canopy of the forest telling me we'd already traveled a far distance from the estate.

"How are we getting to the city?" Thomas asked.

"Car—except for me," Jagger explained, his gaze on me as I tried to hide the anxiety his words caused. Why were we separating now, of all times? "I'm flying ahead to make Linan aware that we've left and to keep an eye out for any other reinforcements he may have coming. When I get within city limits, I'll drop down and travel the rest of the way there on foot."

I knew his plan made sense. I hated the idea of being separated, but I also trusted my mates—and if they thought this was a good plan, I supported them.

"Be safe," I told him as he stole a quick kiss before jogging towards a clearing in the trees. In a swift, practiced movement, he shifted and soared into the air as the rest of us hurried toward the unpaved road nearby. While I couldn't see Jagger above the treetops, I could feel him, and as we got into the dark SUV, my gaze snagged on the estate lit up in the distance.

Stay safe. It was my only wish for all of them—for them to stay safe until we could handle this for good.

Chapter 3

Jagger Silvershade

As I soared above the trees as conspicuously as I could without being suspicious, I kept an eye on the vehicle that made its way down the road that separated the Bronzeheart and Silvershade estates—the SUV that held my precious mate. My treasure.

Rationally, I knew that Bexley was safe—extremely safe—but I couldn't help the paranoia that something bad would happen while I wasn't by her side. It didn't help that I didn't have my mark on her pretty little neck yet, nor her scaled markings on my own. That our bond wasn't complete and etched into us for all of eternity.

Until we were completely tied to one another—until every threat to my mate was truly taken care of, like fucking Clanguard—I would feel uneasy. Even after that I'd probably still be uncomfortable leaving her side.

Unfortunately, Linan made a grievous mistake if he thought for a second we would take this lightly. *Linan would pay for what he'd done and what he planned to do—especially to Bexley.*

Expanding my attention outward to the other two territories, I searched for any sign of reinforcements heading toward the Silvershade estate. After about twenty minutes of flying, I was met with nothing but silence, the landscape calm in the darkness of the night. He hadn't sent troops anywhere else; only to our meeting.

Despite the calm of the clan lands, the city center was anything but. In addition to the normal urban soundscapes, the distant sound of fighting reached my finely tuned ears.

Whether it was related to what was going on or not wasn't something I could tell, but I didn't like not knowing, especially with my mate and my brothers driving right down a central road. Speeding ahead, I swept above the city, drawing looks as I tried to target the source of the loud noise of conflict...only to find a relatively small section to the northeast under attack. Specifically the avian sector, which was closest to the Clanguard pack lands.

Landing on a rooftop, I shifted into my human

form and pulled out my phone, thankful for the magic that allowed me to keep my clothes and personal items on me. It would have been a bitch to constantly carry around and store clothes and other items in caches throughout the territory simply to ensure I wasn't walking around naked. Then again... seeing Bexley shift back without clothes was an appealing thought.

"Jagger, son, is everything okay?" My father answered my call after the fifth ring.

"The avian community is under attack right now —tell Alpha Spencer. I just flew above it and landed to call you."

"I'll tell her," he promised. "Did you see any reinforcements heading our way? I don't have eyes on any, but it's possible they're still leaving the city."

"No reinforcements," I agreed. "It seems Fletcher was right—this was a warning."

"Lay low for the night. We're leaving now, and while I don't see any reinforcements, I have a feeling this is going to get worse before it gets better." My father's voice was thick with concern, and my brows dipped, wondering if we should have left them. I knew they were more than capable of taking care of themselves, but sometimes the enemy could surprise you.

"Agreed." I inhaled sharply. "Both of you stay safe, okay?"

"Of course. I love you, son."

His words caught me off guard as he quickly ended the phone call. I stared down at the phone in thought. I knew my father loved me, but he rarely said it. It wasn't that my family was unaffectionate; my parents were just emotionally reserved, especially around others.

Deciding to send my parents a message saying 'I love you both, stay safe,' I stared at it for a moment longer, wondering if I should call back, before hitting send. I needed to get back to Bexley and ensure she'd arrived at the safe house.

Not waiting for a response, I put away my phone and sprinted to the edge of the building, leaping off and shifting back into my full form mid-air. Soaring above the city once more, I flew toward the southern district before eventually landing in the middle of the street, the area much quieter than the other sector. While street lamps lit up the area, there was no one out, and it gave me the eerie feeling that someone was watching me from the shadows.

Knowing that the SUV had most likely already reached the safe house, I walked several city blocks with my hood up, navigating through alleys to keep out of view as much as I could. When I reached the alley with the SUV parked at the end, I slipped past it and opened the rusted side door to the apartment building. I cringed as I stepped into the stairwell and the door creaked closed—the sound echoing loudly in the night. Shit. Jogging up three flights of stairs, I spotted Breaker outside the door to the hallway, typing away on his phone.

When he looked up, I saw the relief on his face and felt a surge of guilt. I'd been gone longer than what either of them would've considered normal.

"Got lost?" he asked as he stood and stepped into the hallway.

"Had to shift back and call our parents. Clanguard's pack is attacking the avian sector as we speak," I explained, anger seeping into my voice. "I'm not sure why—if it's a simple attack or part of a bigger plan—but it's something we need to keep an eye on as we head toward the pack lands."

"Could also serve as a good distraction," Breaker suggested.

The two of us ducked into the apartment, the doorway shorter than normal, and walked down the steps that created a sunken effect to the unit. The furniture in the place was outdated and dusty, but other than that it was in pretty good condition. I frowned, hating that we weren't at someplace better, a place where Bexley could truly relax.

"Jagger!" Bexley's face filled with a look of relief as she stopped washing down one of the counters to round the dining table and wrap her arms around me. Pulling her close, I buried my nose in her sweet smelling hair as my chest relaxed, warmth radiating through my body at her nearness. There were so many damn emotions the woman made me feel, but this contentment and sense of belonging was like nothing I'd ever experienced before.

"I was so worried when you didn't beat us here," she admitted. Despite her smile, the slight dip in her brow hinted at the concerns weighing heavily on her.

"Something was going on in the avian sector," I explained. "I wanted to give our parents and the council leaders a heads up."

"Oh." Bexley's smile faded as her gaze went momentarily distant. "I hate that. I hate how he seems to be affecting everyone at once—I hate the reach he has."

"I promise you that reach will mean nothing soon," I whispered, kissing her lightly. She sighed into it before pulling away with a small nod, and I watched as she walked back into the kitchen to continue cleaning.

I hated the idea of Bexley lifting a finger...but I also knew she'd want to help everyone else in their attempt to make the place comfortable for the night. I still didn't have to like it though.

"I like this place," Rachel said as she stepped into one of the apartment's four bedrooms. It wasn't much, but safe houses didn't need to live up to our usual standard of living—they just needed the bare necessities.

"It could be really cozy and cute," Bexley agreed as she joined her friend. I approached her, unable to ignore the magnetic pull my mate had on me, reaching her right as her stomach rumbled. Fuck.

Bexley looked up at me with an embarrassed smile as I turned towards the others. "We need food —I'm going to grab some." I was less noticeable and more quiet than the other two.

Thomas nodded towards the door. "I'll go with you. Everyone else should stay here."

"Be safe," Bexley said as I kissed her once more and then set out, trusting Breaker and Gage to keep her safe. I let Thomas lead, and when we finally reached a take-out restaurant lit up by flickering neon signs, I scanned over the menu, ultimately deciding to order one of everything.

Thomas placed a similar order, to the delight of the older woman behind the counter. She offered to have us wait inside the lobby, but we chose instead to sit at a table right outside the restaurant. The clear night sky and silence of the neutral territory once again had me feeling on edge, every single sound making me tense. I almost would have preferred chaos. After the past few days, it would have felt a bit more normal.

We needed tonight to be peaceful, though. We needed a good night's rest before figuring out what our plan was for tomorrow.

"What do you think about all this?" I asked Thomas, curious how he felt now that he was involved in something he'd tried to avoid for so long.

"I have no idea how this is going to end," Thomas admitted, his foot bouncing in agitation. "My father is persistent, and I have a feeling he's never going to stop going after her."

A low, defensive rumble threatened to escape, but I managed to control it. "Even knowing that his two sons are out of his control? I thought the entire point was to have her mate with one of you?" The thought alone made me see fucking red. It made me want to remove Fletcher and Thomas from the equation—forever—despite knowing that they absolutely wanted no part in it.

"Of course, he considers himself a viable option as well," Thomas scoffed.

I had to actively restrain myself as my dragon threatened to break out and cause me to shift, my eyes closing as a scowl of disgust contorted my face. Fucking disgusting bastard.

"Or maybe not." Thomas shrugged. "Maybe it's about control at this point. Maybe any male wolf under his control will do—I'm honestly not sure. I've done my best to remove my father from my life to the furthest extent, stopping only when I thought I would lose my brother. Now that won't be an issue."

"You know Linan is going to die, right?" I wanted to be crystal clear about what was going to happen. While I understood Bexley not wanting others to die and would try to help her with that, Linan was another story.

"He deserves worse than that," Thomas said on a low hiss. "Fletcher and I watched for years as he abused our mother, abused other women, abused pack members—unable to do anything. I got out, and now Fletcher has too, but someone will have to fill the void of power left behind after we kill him. If left alone, one of his followers will, and the situation won't be any better. That's the only snag in all of this. But yes...I'm aware my father has to die."

It felt good to hear him say it. I had trusted them, but his conviction and the venom in his voice were reassuring. At the same time, it didn't completely surprise me. *I* even remembered meeting Linan for the first time at a young age and seeing how he treated his wife, naturally recognizing how wrong it was.

"Son, this is Alpha Clanguard, and these are his sons, Fletcher and Thomas."

I straightened in the presence of another alpha, offering him a hard nod. His eyes flashed with cruel amusement as he met my handshake in a crushing hold, and the longer I looked at him, the more I realized there was something cold and clinical to his gaze. Something that had me turning my attention to his sons instead.

Both of them were staring up at a woman who hadn't yet been introduced. Their mom, I guessed.

"And this is Ca—"

Alpha Clanguard interrupted my mom as she tried to introduce her. "It doesn't matter, at least to you." He offered a dismissive wave without even looking at his wife, ignoring the woman's wounded expression. Both boys shot their father angry looks, which he also completely ignored. "Now, Jagger, you're right around Fletcher's age, right?"

I distinctly remember asking my parents about the interaction later that night, feeling that it was purposefully malicious on his end. My father's response had been to emphasize Clanguard not valuing his mate, but now I realized that the explanation had been the tame, kid-friendly version. I didn't understand then, and I certainly didn't understand now, how a man could treat anyone—let alone his wife, mate, and mother to his children—like that. And for him to want to involve Bexley....

A ding had me looking down to my phone. My parents messaged that they had arrived safely in the Bronzeheart territory, but that some security had stayed behind to show a presence, understanding they were putting their lives at risk. I looked back up to find that Thomas had stood, a bell ringing from the restaurant alerting us that our food was ready.

We grabbed our bags of food and made our way back to the apartment in silence, each of us trapped in our own thoughts. By the time we reached the apartment and locked the door behind us, Bexley had already fallen asleep. Gage was on the couch with her, and Rachel and Fletcher had disappeared. Thomas took their bag of food to them down the hall as I set ours down on the coffee table, Breaker appearing with freshly washed plates and silverware.

"Everything good?" Gage asked.

I nodded. "Tired. Just tired. How's Bex? I wish she hadn't fallen asleep without eating." I felt like we hadn't been able to take care of our mate enough lately, something that made me extremely uncomfortable.

"She was exhausted, fell asleep the minute she sat down," Gage explained, his brows furrowed in concern as he brushed a piece of her golden hair back from her face.

"She should eat," I murmured, though I wasn't willing to wake her up. Instead I fixed myself a plate and sat in a chair diagonal to the couch. They had finished cleaning while we were gone, the windows cracked to relieve the mustiness. Bexley had also changed and showered, her golden hair drying in waves. It was partially pulled back, showcasing her marks from Gage and Breaker.

I forced myself to not feel jealousy over them, knowing that there was a time for everything, and our time would come. Even if recently it felt like we were shorter on time than I would have preferred.

"Everyone made it to the Bronzeheart estate safely," I said, filling them in on my parents' message. "Now we have to figure out how we're going to manage to find her parents."

"The brothers seem to have a good idea of where they are," Gage pointed out, "but I do worry about Linan discovering our intention. If the location is in the pack lands or the main packhouse, our plan includes significant risk. One I am not willing to put Bexley through. I mean, what are the chances that he'll decide to leave now?"

"It's possible he will since our parents gave up the Silvershade estate," Breaker said, his wording making me grimace. "He'll probably want to be there himself to deliver the blow to their ego and pride, so I think there's a good chance we'll only have to deal with whatever forces he leaves at the pack house. After all, why would he assume we'd go there? Why would he assume, after all these years, that we'd know about them being there? He's been playing offensively up until now; I doubt that will change."

"You're right. And the move to our estate would show confidence," I agreed.

"Our biggest obstacle," Fletcher said as he entered the room to grab some extra silverware, "is ensuring we can release her parents from wherever they're contained. It won't be a normal prison. I'm not sure what it will be, but not that. We need to be prepared for the possibility that we don't have the strength or means to release them, even if we locate them."

"If they can't break out of it, why would we be able to break into it?" Gage agreed. "Is it possible that it's a simple lock-and-key situation?"

"Unlikely. It's probably warded or something.

My father has a few friends from the witch sector that have helped him throughout the years—"

A whimper left Bexley's lips, and we all snapped our gazes towards her, panic slamming into my chest at the unexpected tear rolling down her cheek. Surging forward to kneel next to her, I ran my fingers over her face. Her mark on my neck burned, and as I lifted my other hand to it, I was thrown headfirst into Bexley's dreamscape.

Chapter 4

Bexley Blackforge

Drip. Drop. Drip. Drop.

My head pulsated with pain. It was like I'd collapsed and slammed my head on a concrete floor, or like I'd fallen from a high distance onto my back. Everything hurt. So incredibly much. Every bone felt like it was moments away from snapping, and my nerves felt like they were on fire.

Somehow, though, that was only a small aspect of what I was focused on. Instead, my attention was captured by the magic surrounding me, swirling in the air like darkened glitter. I could feel another pull as well, the connection with my mates strong and vibrant, comforting me. It wasn't enough to lessen the pain, but it did distract me.

A groan left my throat as I turned, rolling onto my stomach and pushing myself up to standing. A whimper of pain left my throat as the world spun around me and I stumbled.

Where was I?

My gaze darted around the darkened room as my eyes tried to adjust. The black stone walls of the room were slick with moisture; probably the same unknown liquid that was dripping onto the stone floor. The dampness in the air was palpable, the scent of mold in the confined space nearly suffocating.

Intertwining my fingers, I took a deep breath, wondering what type of dream this was. Clearly not a memory. I'd never been here before.

Drip. Drop. Drip. Drop.

Stepping into the darkness, a rattling of chains had me freezing in surprise. I narrowed my eyes, then rubbed at them when that didn't work. Normally my vision wouldn't have been a problem, but I had a feeling this wasn't true darkness or absence of light. This had to do with magic, the inky black seemingly alive.

"Hello? Is anyone there?" My voice sounded weak.

The rattling of chains silenced, replaced by a deep bass sound that sent an uneasy chill rolling up my spine. My skin prickled, and a vibrant flash of light—like the crackling of electricity—highlighted two figures in the distance, both kneeling with their heads down. It felt like they were at the end of a very long hallway, and on instinct I stumbled back, my heart thumping loudly as a sense of visceral fear built inside of me. The power coming off the two of them was insanely intense.

When the woman lifted her head, I found myself peering into the face of someone I'd seen only in memories. How I had forgotten her, even with magic, was almost unbelievable.

My mother.

"Cupcake." Gage's voice had my eyes fluttering open. I stared up into his bronze gaze, the relief and comfort at his presence only momentary as I was pulled back under by the vision that held me hostage.

My back hit a solid door, but I passed right through it as if I were a phantom. A scream pierced the air, feral and unforgiving. The door shuddered but didn't give way to the woman slamming her body against it with all her might. I whimpered as tears stained my cheeks at the raw agony in every cry. I could feel that she was in pain—both emotional and physical. Despite the danger to me, I surged forward and tried to open the heavy doors that separated her from me.

But I couldn't even reach it, let alone open or pass through it.

Instead, all I could focus on was the black metal block chained between the door handles—connecting them. It sparkled under the dim lighting of the cavern, and I tried to commit the details of it to memory. I knew that this was what would keep me from my parents. This is what would stop me from saving them. I took in every single detail, not willing to wake up, even as the intense magic from the other side caused my nose to bleed. Not until I had enough information to ensure we could rescue them.

"Bexley!" Gage's voice broke through the vision. I flung up, gasping and nearly slamming my head right into Jagger's as he leaned over me in concern. Beads of sweat tickled the back of my neck, and a tremble ran through me. Blood leaked from my nose, and I tried to blink rapidly to clear my eyes of the tears that crowded them. The vision had triggered such an intense physical reaction that I could barely think straight, let alone explain myself.

"Just breathe." Jagger brushed my hair back, and I leaned into his comforting touch. "Your body is reacting to the amount of energy it took to travel like that."

"Travel?" I asked, my voice a hoarse whisper. Whatever had just happened, I really had no intention of it happening again—my heart felt like it was going to beat out of my chest in violent palpitations.

"When you have a connection with someone, the magic that comes from our dragon counterpart allows us to see where they are," Breaker explained. "It isn't an easy connection to make; it takes a lot of physical stamina...but it's a safeguard for our kind. Which is why I felt a hell of a lot better once our mating bond was established because no matter what happened, I knew I'd be able to find you in a dreamscape."

"But how does that apply to my parents?" I frowned. "And wait, how did you know I traveled? Can you see my dreams now?" Because if so, that could get interesting...

"Yes, all three of us can see them. Although because we only have half of a connection, I wasn't able to see nearly as much as the other two—just small snippets. We waited to wake you up until we felt like we'd gotten as much information as we could about the lock," Jagger explained.

"In terms of how it works, parental or sibling bonds can work the same way as the mate bond for that type of tracking, especially because of your shared bloodline," Gage said. "It's the way we protect our own."

"So that was *actually* my parents? Not just a vision?"

"Exactly."

"Why now?" I whispered. "I don't...I don't understand."

"What were you thinking about before you fell asleep?" Jagger asked.

"Them. How much I wanted to find them and if they were okay..." Tears pricked my eyes as I let out a shaky exhale. "I must have somehow called them."

They'd been in *so much* pain. "We have to save them. We absolutely *have* to get them out of there."

"We will," Jagger promised. "We may need some extra help with that lock, though."

I gave him a questioning look as Breaker sat down next to me, pulling me against him as I sought comfort in his touch. "We may need to find a witch willing to help us, or even go to Carmina itself."

My eyes widened at the idea of that, as Gage stood up and walked towards the kitchen. "But before we do any of that, let's get you something to eat."

"Actually, I really could use a shower first," I

admitted. My skin felt clammy in the aftermath of the adrenaline that had rushed through me.

"We'll get breakfast while you shower," Jagger assured me. Giving him a peck on the cheek in thanks, I made my way toward the apartment's singular bathroom, which thanks to Rachel had been recently cleaned. Yesterday it hadn't been particularly fun cleaning the entire place, but now it felt worth it, especially because we were able to relax in moderate comfort.

Closing the door, I made quick work of a shower, making sure to scrub my body and hair. While I'd showered last night, I hadn't wanted to take too long since everyone else had needed to as well, so this time I stole a few extra minutes.

Right as I was about to get out of the shower, Gage slipped in and left a pile of clothes on the counter. I hadn't realized I'd left the door unlocked, but I suppose it was a good thing since I'd forgotten to bring anything in with me...including a towel. I grimaced, ending up using my old clothing to pat off before getting dressed in a pair of dark jeans, black socks, and a hoodie from Jagger that I'd thrown into my bag. It wasn't my normal style, but my normal style tended to attract a lot of attention, so this was probably for the better.

Finding a toothbrush and hairbrush in the pile, I

made sure to brush my teeth and then braided my hair into two long braids down my back before giving myself a once over and exiting the bathroom. Right outside were my sneakers, which I slipped on as I made my way back into the living room, feeling far more settled. Now I was just super hungry.

I sighed happily as the scent of breakfast reached my nose.

My mates were already talking about our plan moving forward, so I sat down and began to eat the plate that Breaker slid in front of me. As I bit into a piece of bacon, the three of them discussed which witch in Trabea or even in the witch sector would be the best to help us open that lock. My brow furrowed as I tilted my head in thought. *Wait, why did we need a witch?* I felt like I was missing a piece of the puzzle —so I asked them to explain.

"The lock had a magical signature that was most likely left by a witch," Jagger explained. "A key isn't going to work. Ideally we'd see if any witches here in the city or in our clan lands could help, but—"

"Can't be local," Fletcher said as he joined us in the kitchen. Rachel and Thomas must have still been sleeping. "Any local witches will likely have an alliance with my father, so we'll need to get word to the witch sector and have someone brought over. Or—"

"Travel there," I suggested, deciding I was a fan of that plan.

"Like I said, ideally we wouldn't have to," Jagger murmured.

"Really hate the idea of that," Gage agreed. I didn't fully understand their reasoning, offering both of them a curious look. Breaker didn't share his opinion, instead just shaking his head.

"It could be helpful for more than one reason," Fletcher countered. "When the portal is used by storm dragons, the effects are felt throughout the city. And if you know what to look for, it isn't hard to tell who's traveling in and out of our territory. So if the four of you travel to the witch sector, it may delay my father from launching further attacks—he'll assume you're running or trying to hide Bexley, and he won't bother wasting bodies on a war that wouldn't result in her capture."

"It's not a bad plan," Breaker admitted.

"The witch territory, though, is..."

"Dangerous," Gage summarized.

"The Nyx family are allies of ours and control large sectors within the territory and city of Carmina, so it wouldn't be hard to find help," Breaker pointed out.

"Why does that name sound familiar?" The name Nyx stood out to me, but I wasn't sure why. I didn't understand the politics in Carmina at all—and I knew I was showing that—but hopefully Fletcher wouldn't judge.

"Grimshaw Nyx goes to school with us in the witch sector," Jagger explained.

"He's one of your friend's mates—we met them the night of the party," Breaker reminded me, causing my brows to shoot up as I remembered the dangerous set of men that had surrounded Deva. "My family is fairly close with them, but I think all the dragon clans have worked with them before."

"But how do we make sure that we'll be able to get back through the portal without incident? How do we know that Linan won't follow us?" Gage asked, interrupting our conversation with a thought of his own.

"We can wait by the portal and keep the area secure until you come back," Thomas suggested. Rachel followed in after him, giving me a hug before taking a piece of bacon from my plate. I would have scowled if Gage hadn't immediately replaced it with one of his.

My dragon wasn't completely happy with that solution, though, because now she was worried that he was more hungry than we were and didn't have enough to eat...

"Plus, when your friend Rebecca returns from

the fae lands, we can point her in the right direction," Rachel added. That seemed to seal the deal with everyone else. I worried about Rebecca coming in light of the chaos erupting, but instinct told me she was more than capable of protecting herself.

"Alright, then we go," Gage said. "I don't like it, but getting distance from Linan is exactly what I want—all the better if it serves our purpose in the long run."

I was never going to say no about traveling to another realm.

"I'm opening it this time!" I announced to my mates as we approached the warehouse that housed the portal. Rachel and her mates were taking a separate car that followed a few blocks behind us so that we didn't attract too much attention. Gage was also making sure to keep to side streets as we passed the pack lands, my foot bouncing as an anxious energy invaded my soul.

"Okay, *mo chuisle*," Breaker agreed. "Although, you know we could just do it together."

"We could, and I love that idea, but I really want to prove to myself that I can do it again—purposefully. Plus, I imagine you'll need to use your magic in the witch sector more than I will. We have absolutely no idea what to expect there or what danger we could face, so I really want to do my part now. I would say I could be part of a potential fight, but..."

"No." Gage's tone was hard. I shrugged, trying to conceal my amusement at his reaction, knowing I'd made my point. "You're right though—there's been a lot of chaos within Carmina lately, and rumor has it that it's surrounding your friend, actually."

"Deva's in trouble?" I asked, stopping in my tracks.

"There's been revolutionary activity throughout the realm, and she and her mates are involved," Gage summarized. "But that's all we know."

"So we need to be on guard," Jagger concluded. I nodded in understanding.

Parking the car in an alley nearby, we got out and made our way silently into the warehouse. The streets surrounding it were quieter than usual as the cloudy skies above seemed to darken in anticipation of our magic.

I'd already said my goodbyes to Rachel, so we didn't wait for them to join us as we once more came face to face with the territory's portal. I studied the worn, handcrafted wood that had been through years —possibly decades or even centuries—of use as the framing for the gateway. Deciding to not second-guess my instincts, I stepped toward the portal and ran my fingers along the smooth wood, pulling on the flame in the center of my chest.

This time I kept my eyes open as, like a spark to gasoline, the frame of the portal erupted in black flames that licked toward the center to create an onyx surface of fire. Outside, winds battered the windows, and electricity crackled through every inch of me.

A sudden flash of lightning lit up the room as a vacuum of power pulled me forward, tugging me away from my mates, through the black inferno and into Carmina.

Chapter 5

Gage Bronzeheart

I pulled Bexley into my arms the moment I emerged from the portal, finding her completely and perfectly fine. When she'd been sucked in without us, I worried that she had somehow been injured, or that I'd find she'd disappeared once I reached the other side. Until this threat was handled, I was constantly fearful that my mate would be taken from me—that she'd just disappear without a word.

But here she was, tilting her head back and staring up at me with wide, beautiful eyes that danced with soft amusement. Letting out a slow exhale, I tugged her under some tree cover as the other two exited the portal behind me. As soon as they were through, our magic recoiled, summoning a dramatic response within Carmina.

There was a stormy atmosphere that was innate

to this realm, but the reaction we caused was something else entirely.

After traveling so much recently we should have been used to it, but I could see the surprise on Bexley's face at the explosion of storm energy that sounded through the air. I looked skyward through the trees, watching the already charcoal skies turn black as lightning crackled through the sky. Wind washed over us in a hurricane-like effect and cold rain pelted our skin, hitting hard enough that it felt like hail, causing me to pull Bexley further into me.

When it finally settled, I let out a frustrated noise, finding that Bexley's hair was soaked and she was shivering slightly. I shrugged off my jacket and wrapped it around her, her lips pressing into a thankful smile that made me want to kiss her. I knew it wasn't the time, but my reason and rationality didn't always work well when it came to my cupcake.

"That felt amazing." Bexley tilted her chin up as I watched her eyes bleed black, her dragon feeding off the intensity of storm power around us. My mate then spun from my arms and walked through the crowded brush, returning to the path, skipping right over several puddles while humming happily. I could see just how much the environment was affecting her mood, and I found that I loved it. After a few minutes of walking, we crested a hill and found ourselves looking out on a forested landscape that dipped into a valley.

The countryside looked like something out of a novel, marred only by the inky spot of the gothic city to the south.

"I can see why it would be dangerous for us to be here too often," Bexley called out as thunder rumbled in the distance.

"Why is that?" Jagger asked curiously, Bexley bouncing on her toes as she looked around the foreign land.

"They're a bit stormy here," she said with a cute smile. I swear, this woman was going to kill me. My fingers twitched to pull her back into my arms, but I managed to restrain myself, not liking how out in the open we currently were. I needed to stay on alert.

"In all senses of the word," Breaker agreed.

I sighed. Unfortunately, he was right. And because of the conflict brewing there, the last thing I wanted to do was go to the city. Which left me with one option—I chose to make a phone call that I knew would come with a price to pay. Eventually. In the short-term, though, it would be worth it and make our time here a hell of a lot easier than having to try to track down someone from the Nyx family.

I pulled my phone out, thankful that it even worked—Carmina wasn't known for its technological prowess. No, the territory seemed to be stuck in a state of perpetual decay, where the poor only grew poorer, suffering while the rich lifted themselves so far above everyone else that they were untouchable. Oddly enough, the revolutionary action going on here wasn't about that—no, that was about something much more complicated.

Pulling up a phone number I'd grabbed from my father before leaving, I let the device ring as I watched my mate pointing out things to the other two, fascinated with what Carmina had to offer. Not for the first time, I felt guilty that my cupcake hadn't had more experiences traveling. After we handled this Clanguard bullshit, that would change. In some ways, I suppose it was better that we hadn't traveled a lot, since now she'd be able to share those experiences with all three of us instead of just my family. That concept made me feel moderately better.

"Hello?" A lighthearted voice chimed through the other end, and I felt a surge of relief that the bastard had actually picked up.

"Leandor, this is Gage—"

"Bronzeheart," he filled in, sounding amused. "Yes your father sent word that you would most likely be calling." Of course he had—I don't know why I would've expected anything different. "To what do I owe the pleasure?"

I was distracted by voices on the other end of the phone in the background, and I considered that this may have been a bad idea. A favor was never free, especially in a place like this. And while Leandor was a friend of the family, I had no idea who he'd aligned himself with outside of the Nyx family.

"If I'm interrupting something..."

"Nonsense." The background noises went silent as the soft *thunk* of a door shutting sounded through the line. "My son and his friends have been causing chaos in the territory, which is nothing new. Unfortunately, because of that I am surrounded by lots of people—all the time."

I'd heard that Cage, his son, had left campus. Considering he was friends with Grimshaw Nyx, whose family essentially ruled the realm...well, it wasn't surprising to confirm that they were part of whatever was going on in Carmina.

"So, how can I help you, Gage?" Leandor finished.

"Right. Well...my mate, myself, and the other two heirs just arrived in Carmina through the main portal—"

"Ah, that was you all! Well, that solves that. Idra—" His voice was a sing-song tone before a long pause, clearly waiting for someone to join him. "Apparently the magical surge was the storm dragon heirs arriving, no need to call anyone," he explained to whoever this 'Idra' was—I was going to assume his wife. "Sorry, go on."

Breaker arched a brow in question, probably at my pinched expression, but I shrugged it off. If it'd been anyone else I would've felt like the constant conversational tangents were disrespectful, but I knew that wasn't the case when it came to Leandor. Their entire family was a bit eccentric, to say the least. While Breaker's family had been in contact with the Nyx's more, Leandor had been my father's point of contact within Carmina for years.

"We need help," I said, keeping it simple. "Two of the storm dragon clan rulers have been imprisoned, and their cell has a lock that's strong enough to keep them contained. We need help figuring out how to break it."

I could practically hear the surprise from the silence on the other end of the line.

"Well, of course. We can't have clan leaders imprisoned," he finally murmured. "And you're at the portal? You haven't traveled toward the city yet?"

"Correct. We're hoping to avoid the city, and we haven't moved far from the portal."

"Perfect. Follow the path three miles north, and when you hit the first town, go to the largest house at the end of the lane—it's one of our country homes.

One of my sons should be there right now; he'll be able to help you if you explain the lock. Most likely, hopefully at least, it's not as complicated as it appears."

"Thank you, Leandor. I appreciate it."

"No problem. If we weren't in the city, we'd join you. But I'm only a call away, so let me know if you need anything else."

After saying goodbye, I hung up and slipped my phone into my jacket, walking towards the others. "We have a direction. Leandor said one of his sons should be able to help. We need to head about three miles north."

"I haven't looked in that direction yet," Bexley hummed as she waltzed past me. Grabbing her around the waist, I tilted her chin up and kissed her in the briefest touch before letting her loose to lead us down the path. Now that we'd announced our presence, I wasn't as concerned about Bexley's safety here, especially since we didn't have to travel into the city.

The thickly forested path stretched on forever, and while Bexley would randomly point out different things, I found myself trapped in thought. Until a question she asked pulled my full attention.

"So what's the deal with Carmina? Who rules it?"

"That's a bit of a complicated question," I said. My family had always ensured the two of us received an extensive education growing up, but we hadn't put much focus on the other territories outside of Trabea. Something that was probably a reflection of my own clan's self-importance in how we regarded shifters compared to others in our realm, if we were being honest. "Carmina, which is both the name of the territory and the city center, is ruled and protected by the Nyx family."

"One of whom is Deva's mate," Bexley summarized. "Got it. That's sort of crazy. Talk about power." Her surprise at Grimshaw's importance had me smirking as the other two offered her amused looks. Bexley often forgot what a similar position she herself was in as the Flash clan heir. "So are they the governing body or..."

"Not officially, and not elected—just the wealthiest and most powerful," I explained. "However, there is a purist group that's attempted to call their power into question. They live in the northern part of the territory, is my understanding, and they've been trying to rid Carmina of unblessed witches and lay claim to the city. I don't know much more about the politics, but the revolutionary activity going on has to do with that particular conflict."

"Wow," she murmured. "The purist group, are they dangerous?"

I knew she wasn't thinking about the danger to herself as we traveled through the territory—she was worried about Deva. My mate was always worrying about everyone but herself, a quality I both loved and one that concerned me greatly.

"Yes," Breaker answered, "although their leader lost his prized assassin years ago, so I'm not sure if that's changed anything."

Bexley's eyes darkened with concern, and I found myself grasping at a way to change topics. "Do you know about the different witch types?"

"You said there are unblessed witches." Bexley frowned. "I feel like I should know what the other types are, but I can't recall if I ever learned them."

She had learned about the types of witches, but the lesson had been on a day when her memory spell had been triggered by information regarding our own realm and a minor conflict between Carmina and Trabea—causing her agonizing pain. She'd probably blocked the entire day from her memory. *Never fucking again* would I allow anyone or anything to hurt her so badly.

"Are there blessed witches?"

"Yes," Jagger answered. "There are three types of blessed witches: lunar, blood, and shadow. Although 'blessed' and 'unblessed' are absolutely ridiculous distinctions. Especially considering that both have magic and the latter simply deals with more natural elements of the world rather than darkness, death, and bloodshed."

"Deva is a lunar witch for sure," Bexley murmured, more to herself than to us.

"How do you know?" I asked.

Bexley looked at me in surprise before tilting her head in thought. "I guess you haven't really seen her outside of the school gathering that Estrid called." And even then I had been wholly focused on monitoring threats and looking at my mate. "I mean, she practically has silver skin, and her hair is literally navy. She has to be lunar. If she isn't, I'd be shocked."

"She is," Breaker confirmed. "After we ran into them, I did a background check on their group, including her. I couldn't find much, but she's listed as a lunar witch in her academic records."

Luckily, Bexley didn't seem to view the infringement of privacy as a problem, nodding contentedly.

"So four types of witches, and there's a group that doesn't want the unblessed witches around," Bexley summarized. "So who's Leandor?"

"Cage's father. His son is one of Deva's mates as well, and his family is an allied family with the Nyx's cause."

"So they're going to help us figure out how to break the lock?"

"That's the plan. He said one of his sons would help, but I'm not sure which it'll be—I believe they have nine in total."

Bexley came to a full stop, her brows shooting up. "Nine boys?! Nine children?!"

"It is a lot," I agreed. "Although female storm dragons have litters, so that could be us one day."

Bexley's eyes grew comically large. "I...I knew that, but somehow the reality is ten times more insane to consider. I mean, how many are we talking, exactly? Surely not more than like three at a time, right?" Her voice squeaked at the end, and I reached over to run a hand on her back in a comforting motion.

"If it helps, I think the last recorded was five at once?" Jagger offered, making Breaker wince. Because let's be honest—there was no way to make that sound appealing. Bexley didn't look scared, though, just shocked.

"Five?" she whispered. "Oh man...that's a lot. I mean, obviously it would be worth it, but I can't imagine that would be a very fun pregnancy."

"Don't worry, *mo chuisle*, we'll figure out a way to ensure you're comfortable no matter what the future brings."

"Deal." Bexley flashed us a wry smile. "But if I do that, I get all the cupcakes I want, even if it means not having real food."

I couldn't help but laugh, not bothering to even pretend to balk at her request because I was absolutely willing to give the woman whatever she wanted. I couldn't imagine denying her cupcakes on a normal day, let alone when she was pregnant.

Before we could continue our discussion about the future, we reached the outskirts of a village that I could tell was our destination. A row of houses sat to either side of the road that led to a large gothic estate at the end of the literal road. Each property had at least an acre of land behind it before hitting the forest line, and I wondered briefly if the entire town was owned by their family.

My suspicion was confirmed as people left their houses, all sporting a very similar set of crimson eyes. Kids gave us curious looks, and some of the women were waving to us. I noted a distinct lack of men in the village, and I wondered who was watching over it. Then again, Leandor did say one of his sons would be here, and more importantly...I knew that mindset was more than a bit archaic. These women and even children could probably protect themselves against us, let alone other witches.

"They seem friendly," Bexley said. It was probably because they all belonged to one of the most powerful families of blood witches in Carmina, meaning they had nothing to fear from us. As much as I hated to admit it, we'd probably be at a disadvantage in a fight. While we fought with brutal force, blood witches barely had to lift a finger to inflict damage on a large scale. It was what made them terrifying.

"Blood witches at the top of their game can remove every ounce of liquid from your body with a singular snap of their fingers, so I have a feeling they don't view us as threats."

"Seriously?" Bexley asked, her eyes wide with intrigue and a bit of disgust pinching her face. "I'm... I don't think I like the idea of having that type of magic around me, let alone being able to do something like that."

"Yes, they are an...interesting group," I admitted. I had a lot more words I wanted to use to describe blood witches, but now was not the time for that. Especially if we wanted help from anyone in this village—I had a feeling they could hear everything we were saying.

When we reached the estate at the end of the road, the door opened to reveal a man in his mid-thirties, his red gaze running over all four of us with a look that somehow managed to be both curious and disinterested. It certainly wasn't a friendly look...but it also wasn't *not* friendly. It felt like we'd interrupted his day, which considering the short notice was likely true.

"You must be the dragons," the person said. "My father called to tell me you'd be coming by. Please come in."

"The dragons," Breaker chuckled under his breath. "That's a new one."

Keeping Bexley between us, we entered the shadow-filled home, the wards passing over us like a veil slipping over our skin. I looked around as we made our way past a formal sitting area with luxurious furniture, appreciating the intricate woodwork and candlelit surfaces. We followed the man down the hall into an office, and I was surprised to find a woman there with two one-year-old tots sitting on the floor.

"I'm not sure if my father mentioned who would be helping you, but the name is Moloch, and this is my wife Calliope—along with our two daughters, Belinda and Mara." His wife stood as the babies continued to play on the floor.

"Welcome to our home. Have you eaten yet? I

can make something." She kept her gaze directly on Bexley, and I could tell it was something my mate appreciated. Her dragon could be possessive when it came to other women. Something I fucking loved, if we were being honest.

"I will never say no to food, but *only* if it isn't a hassle," Bexley said, emphasizing the last part.

"No problem at all," Calliope insisted happily and slipped from the room.

Almost immediately my mate was on the floor with the babies, smiling as they played with little toys—wooden moons and suns.

"So how can we help you?" Moloch asked, leaning against the desk. Despite looking at us, I could tell he was focused on his children. I didn't think he viewed Bexley as a threat, but there were also four strangers in his house, so I didn't blame him for his caution.

"We need to release two storm dragon clan leaders being held captive. The pack that put them there used magic either on the lock or to create the lock—we've seen it," I explained.

"You have a distinct memory of this lock?" he asked as he went to a glass cabinet, taking out what appeared to be a smoky dark orb.

"In a dreamscape, yes," Jagger agreed.

"And who experienced it firsthand? Whose dream was it?"

"Me." Bexley stood as he set the orb down on the desk, and Moloch motioned for her to join him.

"This orb can take an imprint of your dream. Once that's done, I can start the process of trying to figure out what type of magic we need to counter this lock of yours."

"It's that easy?" Breaker mused.

"Far from it, but my father is eager to have a stronger alliance with the storm dragon clans, so we will do what we can." As Bexley placed her delicate hands on the orb, we kept our distance but stayed close enough to grab her if needed. "Now," he said to Bex, "find the place in your memory where the dream is stored. Play it through your mind. The orb will do the rest."

Bex closed her eyes, and I could sense the magic in the air as the orb tugged at the memory. My mate's frame swayed as the orb began to flash with bright colors, displaying snippets of the dream we'd experienced. After only a few seconds, the orb darkened as Bexley dropped her hands and blinked, looking slightly dazed. I took a step toward her, but Bex was gone before I could get to her. One of the little girls had started to cry, and Bexley immediately darted over to soothe her.

Clearly having decided he could trust Bexley and content that his daughter was in good hands, Moloch placed the orb in front of himself, his fingers tracing over it before he closed his eyes, getting a read on the dream himself. Bexley let out a soft hum and rocked the little girl in her arms as the other continued to stack her blocks. It was such a domestic scene that I'd nearly forgotten what we were doing when Moloch broke the silence.

"It's a powerful lock—a power drain. So it's not the lock itself that's keeping these two individuals imprisoned, but rather the spell that's making them so weak they can't leave. Good news is that I have a way to break it."

Thank fuck.

Bexley sighed in relief as a visible weight was lifted from her shoulders. I was thrilled with the news, but I also knew there was no way that it was that simple—it never was.

"It's going to take me about twelve hours to prepare, though. I assume that's okay?"

I nodded in resignation. "Not ideal, but we can make it work."

"Good. Now let me show you to our guest house while dinner is being made," Calliope said from the door. Bexley turned and smiled, the little girl in her arms reaching out for her mother. I had a feeling that despite everything going on, Bexley was absolutely okay with staying an extra night.

It was probably needed before the chaos that would erupt when we arrived back in Trabea—to the war that awaited us.

Chapter 6

Bexley Blackforge

"This is absolutely delicious," I told Calliope as I scooped up the last piece of roast on my dinner plate. I usually preferred sweet foods, but I couldn't deny that the warm explosion of flavors that accompanied the dish was absolutely memorable.

It was probably one of the best dishes I'd ever had, which was saying something given the amount of restaurants I'd been to with Celine Bronzeheart and the chefs that'd been brought to the estate. Calliope's cooking was easily better than most of those experiences. And while the setting of the formal dining room was exactly that—formal—the atmosphere was *anything* but.

The couple's two little girls were cooing happily while smearing food on each other's highchair trays and their own hands and arms, the tiny gap between their seats doing very little to stop them. Music played from the kitchen, the clattering of dishes suggesting that the men were done eating as well. They'd chosen to sit in there so they could talk about the politics of the realm. While I did find that interesting, I was way more fascinated by Calliope's dynamic with her two children.

I hadn't been around babies very often, and I was captivated by their adorable faces and chubby little cheeks, especially when they smiled at you. Calliope handled them with so much ease, responding to what they needed in a way that seemed instinctual. It made me hope that when my mates and I had kids, I would be able to slip into that role just as easily.

"I'm glad you like it," she said with an authentic smile, her eyes filling with pride. "It's been hard to cook as much since the twins were born—I only finally got back into it a month or so ago. It used to be something I did daily, multiple times a day."

"Too much with the little ones demanding so much attention?" I guessed.

"That...and I sort of just lost the inspiration to after they were born—until they started eating. Now it feels more purposeful since they can eat most anything I fix. When they were first born, the days felt so exhausting and long, and the weeks even longer, so the last thing I wanted to do was *also* cook.

But now that they're moving around on their own and are a little more independent, I feel like I've got some freedom during the day."

I nodded in understanding, as if I could comprehend what it was like to be a mom. I was out of my depth, but I tried to respond honestly. "I can't imagine what it's like to be a mom, but you've clearly got it down—they are absolutely obsessed with you. They light up every time they hear your voice."

Calliope looked down at them, her happy smile in return making one of them giggle. "That's one of the amazing things about babies—they look at you like you're their entire world. Heals a little part of me every time, I won't lie. And having double that with twins? It makes it slightly easier on the more chaotic days."

"Female storm dragons normally have litters, so I imagine I'll eventually be in a similar position," I murmured in thought, my gaze moving to the window for a long moment. When I looked back at Calliope, her eyes were wide with surprise. I had noticed that she and the babies had the darkest brown eyes—nearly black—whereas Moloch's were crimson. The twins though had a mix of the warm golden brown tones in their hair from him alongside the raven black shade that she sported.

Both Calliope and Moloch were beautiful, but in

a way that was unusual and almost painful to look at —like they were shining just a bit too bright. Like their life force was just a bit too intense for the normal person to experience comfortably. I had a feeling it was a result of their magic; its way of warning others that they were dangerous.

"A litter? Fates, I thought two was a lot. How many are in a litter?"

"Last one had five, apparently." I winced as she hissed through her teeth.

"Shit." Calliope's curse and following laugh had me shrugging with an amused smile. "Well, you'll totally know exactly what I'm talking about when the time comes. Although do yourself a favor and make sure you have a ton of help on hand—some people view accepting help as a weakness, but that's ridiculous. There's no built-in manual for this type of thing, so don't *ever* worry about asking. I'm lucky enough to live by his family; if it wasn't for them there would have been a lot of very long days."

"Luckily we have a lot of very close family too," I said with a happy sigh. For just a moment I noticed my words caused a tinge of sadness to fill her expression before she completely extinguished it. "What about you? Did you have any of your own family come by?"

"Oh, I don't have any family," she said, her

demeanor changing as her eyes darted away. "I was raised in an orphanage up north, so no one of note."

I couldn't imagine what that must be like. Sure, I'd spent most of my life thinking my parents had died, but I had the Bronzehearts to take care of me, and they treated me as one of their own. Calliope was clearly uncomfortable, so I decided to change the topic. "So, where'd you learn to cook?"

Calliope noticeably relaxed. "When I started working in the city, I needed to make my groceries last. Plus, it was some fun after a long day of work."

"Well I'd love this recipe. I don't cook often, but I wouldn't mind trying my hand at it."

Her eyes lit up. "Absolutely." Then we both broke into laughter as one of the babies threw a piece of food right into my hair. After that we both started to pick up and bring the dishes into the kitchen, making sure to wipe the babies down. I felt oddly at home here, comfortable and content to help with the cleanup and the children. Of course it helped that we had already received the tour of the estate, including the guest house in the back where we would be staying.

I hadn't hesitated to compliment both of them on their home during the tour, the entire gothic manor imprinting in my mind. While it wasn't my normal style, I loved the luxurious but moody vibe that matched the constant state of stormy weather here—something I was told was the territory's natural climate rather than a result of our presence. Although we did appear to intensify it, the rain now pouring heavily down on the slate patio out back. It managed to charge up my magic like none of the other realms had, like electricity was running under my skin.

I'd been to three other realms now, and I couldn't lie...this was possibly my favorite. Maybe after all of this was handled I could visit Deva here—or maybe we would get a vacation home here. *That was a fantastic idea!*

After we cleaned up, I stood next to Jagger in the kitchen, his hand rubbing up and down my back as I melted into him. Calliope had already taken the girls to bed, which left me, my mates, and Moloch.

"We can stay up for a while," Gage offered when Moloch mentioned getting back to work.

"I would appreciate the company," he admitted. "It's going to be a long night."

"Bex, you should get some rest," Breaker suggested.

Jagger kissed the top of my head. "I'll head back with you. I'm more tired than I would've expected." Hearing he was tired sent my dragon into overprotective mode, and I found myself bidding the others goodnight as I clasped Jagger's hand in mine, dragging him out of the house and towards the guest house.

"I promise I'm okay, little treasure. More of an excuse to spend alone time with you than anything," Jagger said, chuckling.

I narrowed my eyes on him. "My dragon doesn't believe you. This situation is draining all of us, and at the end of the day, this is turning into a war. One that we need to at least be well rested for."

"I don't disagree," Jagger murmured, squeezing my hand since our fingers were intertwined. "The Clanguard wolf pack has turned this into a rather lethal affair."

It was indisputable, and I hated it.

As we reached the guest house, Jagger broke the thought-filled silence. "What's on your mind?"

"I think I'm just trying to imagine what life will be like after this. I'm ready to get back to some sense of normality, but I don't even know what that means. I don't know if we're going to continue at the academy, or if we want to immediately start leading the clans, and what are we going to do about the Flash clan's old territory?"

"Hey." Jagger swept me into his arms as we stepped into the guest house, pressing his lips to mine. The single-story home had a large central living area and two bedrooms in the back with a shared bathroom. It was comfortable and cozy, the perfect place to spend the night. It also provided us with the perfect amount of privacy we needed right now. "First of all, I love your trust in us. That you don't doubt this will work out."

"I know we'll win, but I'm worried about the cost."

"I know, and I wish I could assure you that there wouldn't be any cost—any lives lost—but already it's happened. We will do our best, I promise you, Bex."

"I believe you, Jagger, I really do."

"Secondly." He gently placed me down in front of the fireplace, which was still crackling from when it'd been lit during our tour. I leaned into him, inhaling his amazing peppermint scent. After hugging me close, Jagger tilted my head back, his rough hands pressed to either side of my face as his gaze traced my features.

"I promise you, everything is going to work out. Every single thing. Nothing else is acceptable. So rest easy knowing we will handle this and everything after. If you want to finish school, then that is exactly what we will do, no questions asked. If you don't want to, then we can focus on reestablishing the Flash clan. If you're not sure, we can take a rest while our parents handle things. We have time."

"We have forever," I said, more as a reminder to myself than to him.

"Forever to love you." His lips dipped against mine. "I love the sound of that, little treasure."

"I love you so much."

"It can't possibly be as much as I love you," he teased, his voice rougher than normal, lifting me up and carrying me toward the larger bedroom in the back. I wrapped my arms around his neck and my legs at his hips, and when he plopped me down on the bed, I stretched out, my arms above me.

A rumble left Jagger's throat, and a flash of darkness that I only ever saw when he and I were alone rolled out from the more civil façade he usually wore. The heat in his normally cool eyes had me squirming. "Fates—you are absolutely beautiful."

When his hand came out to touch my cheek in a soft yet possessive hold, lightning flashed outside, and the wind from the open window blew out the candle on the nightstand. Both Jagger and the storm electrified my skin, and I found myself reaching out to him before I consciously knew I was doing so.

Jagger bent down and met my lips in a hard kiss that was demanding yet sweet, like he was pulling on every ounce of my need for him at once, trying to coax it out but also possessively taking it as his own. I shivered at the intensity of it, and when his fingers smoothed my waist and tugged my shirt up, I helped him slide it off of me, leaving me in a silk bra and my jeans.

"Fuck," he groaned, kneeling on the mattress and leaning over me, trailing kisses between my breasts before moving over the silky material. I arched off the bed with a moan as he circled my hardened nipple with his tongue, wetting the silk before tugging the material away—the delicate flesh feeling like it was on fire as he began to toy with it.

My hands came up to his chest as I tried to pull at his shirt, but with a warning rumble, he took both of my hands captive in one large grip and pulled them above me. Jagger turned his attention to the other breast as I tried to shift, needing some type of friction from him, but his other hand stilled my hip in a commanding move.

"Don't," he warned. "You only get to come if I say so—I want you absolutely dripping before you slide onto my cock—then you can come. *Only* then. Understand?"

"Yes, Jagger." My voice was breathy, and a satisfied rumble left his chest. I cried out as he went back to teasing my skin, and I almost climaxed from that alone, a tremble working its way through my body. When he released my hands and sat back, tugging off his shirt, my eyes roamed over every inch of skin. He was so insanely muscular it was absolutely unreal—he looked like a marble statue come to life.

Hard like one also.

"Stand. Now." His tone did absolutely everything for me, and I hastened to follow his instructions. He spun me so I faced the bed, his rough hands sliding around to unbutton my jeans and then slide them down over my ass. As he knelt to help me step out of them, I knew he could see, and probably scent, just how wet I was.

Jagger pressed a hand to the small of my back, the pressure of his fingertips encouraging me to bend over. When his nose brushed my inner thigh, I let out a moan that had him nipping at my skin as he tugged the wet silk to my ankles.

"You're so wet," he groaned. "I want to slide into you so fucking deep, little treasure."

"Please do." I gasped as his tongue ran along my slit, and my knees nearly broke. When he hardened his tongue and began to fuck me with it, I gripped the bedding and fell forward, letting it catch my weight. Jagger's hands held tight to my hips as he began to devour me, causing my eyes to squeeze shut as I sought the relief that was so close.

"Jagger!" A moan of his name left my lips as he suctioned his lips around my clit and I came hard. Hard enough and explosive enough that I saw stars, my vision turning spotty as shivers erupted all over my skin.

"Fuck. I didn't want you to come yet, but it's so fucking beautiful when you do."

Before I could catch my breath, I was being rolled over, and a feral noise left Jagger's throat as he looked over my naked frame. My legs fell open as he unzipped his jeans and kicked them off, followed by his boxers, his massive length hard and ready. A shiver of anticipation rolled over me as he crawled onto the bed, capturing one leg and pulling it over his shoulder.

A whimper of need left me as the head of his cock brushed over my wet heat, and I fought the urge to beg him to push inside of me, afraid he would play a teasing game. But it seemed Jagger was as impatient as I was because he captured my chin with one hand so I had to hold his gaze while impaling me in one hard thrust.

My scream filled the house as he slid so deep into me my eyes rolled back. His fingers slid over my still sensitive clit, moving in a way that had me both melting and tightening in anticipation.

"I can feel you tightening around me," he groaned, holding himself deep inside of me. "You feel so damn good. I almost don't want to move— want to fucking stay in you forever."

"Please move," I whimpered, lifting my hips. Jagger grunted, somehow pushing further into me.

"I can never deny you," he admitted, his voice a raspy whisper, as he began to pump in and out of me in hard, demanding strokes. The position we were in allowed him to get as deep as he possibly could, my nails digging into the skin on his arms. The faintest scent of blood filled the air, and as he began to stroke faster and faster, the erotic sound of our bodies meeting filled the space. Outside, lightning flashed, illuminating the intense, possessive expression on Jagger's face above me, and the thunder in the distance echoed every movement.

The faster he went, the more it felt like we were racing towards something so much bigger than just our climax. It felt like all my magic was surging and surrounding us in a cyclone as I stared up into his icy eyes. I could practically see a silver glow surrounding him, and for just a moment, I felt our dragons connect, a gigantic crash of thunder sounding outside.

"Shit," he groaned. "I'm going to come—going to come right inside of you."

"Please," I begged. Jagger growled, the sound echoing through the room as he punched his hips forward, slamming into me in one final thrust. His lips came down on the unmarked side of my neck, a gasp of relief escaping me as his teeth sliced into my flesh.

Absolute pure connection surged through me.

Jagger's name left my lips as our bond coated itself in pure silver. Thunder crackled outside, rain pelted down, and lightning lit up the room. Something nearby crashed, and gale-force winds rushed around us. Jagger shielded me with his form, his arms creating a cage above my head as he sank deeper into me. My nails broke skin on his back as his teeth released my neck, allowing me to turn my head to look up at the ceiling.

All at once, it wasn't just our connection.

My own magic swelled inside of me, and the reserve of magic collected from each completion of my mating bond exploded out. The room went dark as my eyes snapped shut, my three metallic mate bonds intertwining with one another in a hard, solid rope. I whimpered at the intensity of it as a pathway of communication opened between all of us—one I hadn't even realized was supposed to be there.

I could feel each of their intense emotions, affections, and even residual elements of their thoughts. I could feel their love for me. A wave of euphoria washed over me, my body radiating with pleasure as lights flashed behind my eyes, my body lying limp under Jagger in a puddle of pure happiness.

It was nearly transcendent.

It wasn't until Jagger held me under warm water that I realized we were in the shower, my body melted against his. Tilting my head up, I found him smiling down at me, his eyes filled with a possessive thread of darkness that he couldn't hide. Letting out what I swear was a purr, I rubbed against him, running my nose against his neck as he picked me up so I was locked against his body.

I didn't even have the energy to tell him I loved him, but I heard him whisper the words, and they were enough for my brain to give into the sleep it was demanding.

If only I realized I would be greeted by dreams on the other side...

Towering walls with cages on all sides surrounded me, the bars triple the width of a person with glowing wards surrounding them. A pair of doors stood at the far end of the corridor, and I knew in that moment what I was seeing.

The exact location of my parents.

Chapter 7

Bexley Blackforge

"This sphere will act as an explosive. It will detonate on the lock and work much more efficiently than trying to make some damn key that may or may not work—especially since we can't get eyes on the inner mechanism," Moloch reasoned. "Of course I could have made a shapeshifting key, but the witch who created the lock probably thought of that and found a way to ward against it. Too risky."

"So brute force," Breaker said. The witch nodded and handed each of us a sphere, their light blue-to-black ombre contents swirling as if they contained shimmering liquid. The spheres were small, but the magic radiating from them gave no doubt that they were powerful.

"How do they work?" Gage asked. "Similar to grenades?"

"And how do we know they're strong enough?" Jagger asked.

Moloch's serious expression turned amused. "First, it's not truly just brute force—they contain an agent that will neutralize wards once they are destroyed, so they can't be rebuilt in the same place. Oftentimes a ward can be blasted through, but then will rebuild and seal on its own. This will ensure that doesn't happen. Secondly, there's nothing stronger in terms of explosives like this. If they don't work, then nothing will. Especially with how they're triggered."

"I definitely want to know that," I said. I didn't consider myself particularly clumsy but...better safe than sorry. I was hoping I couldn't detonate it by accidentally dropping it or tripping while I held it or something equally as ridiculous.

I was leaning against Jagger, my back to his front and his hands resting on my hips. Breaker and Gage were on either side of me and had been most of the morning. I had no doubt they were trying to be mindful of how Jagger would be today with our newly formed mating bond, but they were always right within reach.

I could also feel a sense of newfound content-ment between all of us—as if we were finally exactly how we were meant to be.

When I'd woken up this morning, gray light

filtered through the windows, announcing that it was still very early—dawn at most. Before I'd even had a chance to check the time and confirm, a knock on the door woke all of my mates. Jagger was wrapped tightly around me, his head on my stomach, and the other two were on either side of me. They must have slipped into bed sometime after I'd fallen asleep.

At the knock, Gage had roused himself from bed, returning to tell us that Moloch had arrived. His solution to our lock problem was ready.

I had to admit I'd felt a sense of relief. While I loved the little break we'd had, I was anxious to free my parents and get back home. There was no true relaxing when you knew there was a war waiting for you.

"There are two ways to trigger it," Moloch explained. "The first involves charging it with your power—mostly easily done while traveling through the portal. Because of the high combustion of power that occurs during portal travel, the sphere should light up with enough power to turn silver. At that point you place it where you want it and surge magic through it from afar, similar to any other explosive."

Okay, that seemed pretty easy and not too dangerous.

"And the other way?" Gage asked.

"The other way requires a bit more coordination.

If the portal travel doesn't do it, then the four of you will need to fill the reserves up yourselves. It would take longer, of course, so it may not be the best solution. If you could find a way to bring your powers together into one blast, you would do that and direct it toward the sphere. From there it functions the same."

It was completely possible for them to bring their powers together—I had seen it in action, but as I rolled the small sphere in my hand, I had to wonder if *it* would be powerful enough.

"Just how explosive are these?" Jagger asked, holding his ball up between thumb and forefinger. "If the cages are underground, we don't want to bring down everything on us." I winced at the thought.

"Don't use more than one at a time and you should be okay," Moloch said after a long moment of thought. "Outside of that, the blast radius is concentrated and direct enough that it should have the intended effect. Trigger it from at least fifty feet away also, if possible."

"Understood," Breaker said. "We'll get ready and leave your family be, then."

"Thank you for letting us stay the night," Gage added, Jagger nodding before placing his chin on top of my head, pulling me closer.

Moloch shrugged. "Just remember to pick up the phone when my dad inevitably calls you."

"Of course," Jagger agreed.

"Right." Moloch walked back towards the door. "I'm going back to bed—good luck with everything, and please see yourselves out."

"Thank you!" I called as he walked out, leaving us to get ready.

Deciding I didn't need a shower, I left the boys to pack up as I quickly got dressed, pulling my hair back into an intricate braid and brushing my teeth. Slipping on a pair of dark sparkly leggings and a soft sweater tunic that fell to mid-thigh, I tugged on my jacket and shoes from yesterday. When I opened the bathroom door, I was unsurprised to find Jagger standing there.

My eyes ran over the scale pattern of my mark on him, and my fingers rose to trace the mark he'd placed on my neck. A deep rumble left his throat. My head tilted back as he approached, slipping an arm around my waist.

"You ready?"

"To find my parents?" I felt a rush of excitement and nervous energy. "I hope so...last night I had another dream of where they are. Their exact location. I have no doubt about it now; we just have to figure out how to get there."

"We've got that part covered. And remember, your friend and the Clanguard brothers will be there to help us." He led me to the door of the guest house where the other two were waiting. As we stepped outside, I pulled my jacket tighter around me, shielding myself from the crisp breeze. I nervously put my sphere in the inside pocket, wanting to keep it hidden but within reach. Our group was comfortably silent as we set off down the main street, the neighborhood peacefully still as everyone slept.

Intertwining my fingers with Jagger's on one side and Gage's on the other, I watched as Breaker walked ahead of us, scanning the route, his golden hair damp from the drizzle of cold rain. It wasn't long, though, before I couldn't take it anymore and broke away from Jagger and Gage to pull up his hood...well, *try* to pull up his hood. He had to bend slightly to let me do it, but I felt much better afterwards. When I turned back to check on the others, Gage was on his phone, typing away.

"Any updates?" I asked.

"No." He frowned. "I wanted to give our parents a heads up that we'll be returning to the area, but they haven't responded or picked up my calls. But they'll be able to feel the portal being used, so hopefully that will suffice."

"I'm worried that we don't know what we're

walking into. Or that we were wrong and Clanguard decided to stage an attack," I said, my voice pitching higher than usual with panic. "Do we know if he's moved to the Silvershade estate? We know the clan leaders are safe, but outside of that, we don't know anything."

"We're almost positive he's moved to the estate. The last update we received said specifically that. Of course it's sending the entire territory into panic considering the towns within the Silvershade lands that could be affected, but it also serves our purpose."

"Allows us to know exactly where he's at and to keep eyes on him in a place where we know the land and have plants already placed," Jagger said. "Even if our portal is something he senses, he won't have time to make it back before we've already left the area. Plus, once we get back into Trabea, we'll wait to get confirmation to ensure that we can safely move about —that we have his exact location before leaving city limits."

"I hate that he's taken your home," I said, my throat thick with emotion.

"My home is with you. Don't worry about it, little treasure." His words normally would have had me smiling, but this time I couldn't muster it fully. It didn't change the fact that Clanguard had taken something from my mate. I'd help him get it back in whatever way I could.

As we traveled down the path toward the portal, my three mates talked casually about what Moloch had told them about the realm, but my attention was only half on their conversation. Instead, I was focused on how we'd gotten to this point.

Only weeks ago I was content in a bubble, believing that I would only have Gage at the academy—that I was barely a shifter. Now I not only was a storm dragon, but also a storm dragon *heir* with three mates. I had an entire history I'd been forced to forget, and I had parents that I now knew were still alive.

It was almost insane to consider, and I was so incredibly glad my mates were by my side through this. I wasn't sure I would've been able to do any of this without them, especially considering Clanguard's intentions for me.

"I love all of you," I said, practically blurting the words out in a rush, needing to say them. I didn't understand why it suddenly felt so essential but it did. Their conversation came to a halt as they all turned to me, a blush warming my cheeks.

"And we love you," Gage said, squeezing my hand.

"When all of this is done, I promise we'll have

some normality and be able to fully enjoy it," Breaker promised.

"It's going to be amazing," I agreed, looking up into Jagger's gaze and melting at the love shining there.

It felt right to tell them that I loved them, especially before we stepped into Trabea again.

* * *

The portal felt different this time. As soon as I stepped in I wanted to turn around. My magic felt like it was being directed back into me rather than expanding out the way it usually did. A spark ignited against my chest, making me know it had to do with the sphere in my pocket. My eyes shut for a singular moment, stunned and overwhelmed by the magic around me, before fresh air slammed into me—my body flinging forward and collapsing to the ground...*almost.*

Breaker caught me in his arms as a lethal sound resonated from his chest, so incredibly deadly that fear spun within me even though I knew without a doubt that it wasn't directed toward me. I could feel Gage and Jagger nearby, and when I opened my eyes, feeling disoriented, I found them standing in front of Breaker and me defensively.

"Well, well, who do we have here?"

My metaphorical hackles rose at the voice I unfortunately knew very well now.

Linan. Clanguard.

Straightening myself up, I looked past my two large mates to find the man standing feet away, arms crossed and a cocky smile on his face. That alone would have been enough to make me furious, but behind him I could see that Rachel and her two mates—Linan's own sons—were slumped unconscious against the wall. Metal cuffs restrained them, and their faces were marred by blood, cuts, and darkening bruises.

"Rachel," I cried, hoping she would open her eyes, but the effort was useless.

"She was the first to pass out from the pain," Linan sneered. "What a weak mate my sons chose—unsurprising, though, considering how their mother turned out."

Before I could stop myself, I surged to my feet, only to be stopped by Gage who caught me around my waist and refused to let go. A growl erupted from between my clenched teeth, and I saw Linan hesitate for just a moment before plastering on another amused expression.

"Smart of you to stop her. I have people everywhere."

"Clearly you have spies everywhere as well," Gage observed. "I should have guessed you'd figure it out."

"I'm surprised you didn't follow us," Jagger admitted.

"Why would I do that when all of Trabea is under my control now?"

I tensed and narrowed my eyes. "You don't have control over any—"

"Sure I do," Linan interrupted, silencing me. I fought the urge to let my dragon break out, his disrespect weighing so heavily that it was almost impossible to stay safely still. "All of this was orchestrated perfectly. I don't know what help you assume you found in the other territories, but I can assure you it will be completely and absolutely useless. The only thing you managed to do was get yourself, your mates, and my sons all in the same area. You made my job easier for me, Bexley."

I stayed silent, refusing to rise to the bait.

"Obviously you aren't as smart as your own parents were."

I was on my feet before I even realized it, breaking free from Gage's hold, but before I could reach Linan an electric shock slammed into me. I gasped, dropping hard as I began to convulse, and I heard the buzz of electricity hit my mates before it struck me once again. Linan's men ambushed us with their tasers, my eyes closing as I twitched and power was leached from my body.

A roar broke out as one of my mates tried to shift. I tried to speak, but my voice cracked, so I redirected my efforts into communicating through our bond. *Don't. Don't shift. Not yet.* It was all I could manage before consciousness all but slipped away, leaving me in a haze. Only distantly aware of the world around me.

I came to moments later as another roar sounded, shaking the floor. One of my mates had been hit again. Gathering just enough energy to move my arm, I wrapped my arms around myself protectively, whimpering as something cold and metal collapsed around my wrists. Tears slipped from my eyes, and blood dripped from my nose as another electric shock hit me.

My body was numb at this point.

Linan's hot breath assaulted my ear, his voice unhinged. "Don't you worry, Bexley. We'll make sure you're locked up and able to get well acquainted with my son, even if we have to keep you in here until the next Black Moon."

The sound of a metal grate opening was the last thing I heard before I was overcome by darkness, suffocating any light, noise, or air.

Chapter 8

Breaker Firespell

It took every ounce of my control to not slaughter Linan.

Honestly, I had no idea how I was conscious in the first place. Numerous bolts of electricity had been aimed at me, one specifically finding its target right at the center of my chest. But because I was still conscious, I had to actively stop myself from retaliating. At least until I had a better handle on our current situation.

I'd only woken a minute or two ago when I was dragged out of a vehicle. We were obviously in the pack lands now, but the industrial complex we were being led into wasn't one I recognized. I thought I knew this city, but now I was second-guessing myself —another reason I wasn't willing to fight right now. I didn't have enough strength to stand up straight, let alone free myself or the others.

And I wouldn't risk being separated from my mate until I was certain I could get us out of here successfully.

It also concerned me that I was the only one that was currently conscious.

Bexley was being held by one of the security guards, her head lolled back and eyes shut. Her brow occasionally dipped, but that was the only sign of life. Fury at the way she was being treated—at the asshole holding her and maneuvering her far too fucking roughly—was almost enough to break me from the haze.

I didn't know what type of magic they'd used to drain our power, but while I could feel my flame coming back to life...it was slow. Not how it was supposed to be. My dragon rumbled inside my chest, but it was weak. I didn't think I could shift even if I tried, which was shocking since I'd done so while far more physically injured than I was now. I didn't allow the thought to discourage me, though.

Linan had won this battle, but he wouldn't win the war.

The bastard had specifically instructed my mate to be carried, while the others were damn near dragged along. Gage, Jagger, Fletcher, and Thomas were being pulled by pairs of security guards who struggled against the men's boneless, unconscious weight. Their plight would have been amusing if it wasn't my own brothers getting beat up in the process. Bexley's friend Rachel was hanging over the shoulder of one of the guards, one of her arms twisted at an angle like it was broken.

Frankly, I was surprised Linan hadn't just left her behind in the portal warehouse, but knowing the bastard, he probably planned to use her in his fucked up games to get Fletcher and Thomas to cooperate.

I trudged forward, my limbs heavy as I followed the guard through a pair of metal doors that opened to reveal a darkened space. It looked like a cargo elevator. It was possible it was something else—my vision was still spotty—but it was my best guess.

My dragon roared in protest as I stepped inside, vehemently against being trapped in the relatively small space. I had to go, though. If Bexley was going, then I sure as fuck was going.

Linan joined us and I stared down at him with disdain, refusing to meet the challenge in his gaze. I wouldn't give him the fucking satisfaction.

"Not so tough now. Just wait till you're locked up and your power is being drained constantly." I could hear the victory ringing clear in his voice, and I couldn't wait to extinguish it. I just had to be patient.

Fighting back the impulse to either roll my eyes or rip his fucking head off, I took a steadying breath. Not only for the safety of my mate and my brothers, but because there was something that had been trying to break through the fuzziness in my head— something that told me that this may be exactly what we wanted.

This exact outcome of being imprisoned.

Which of course sounded mental until I remembered *where* he planned to imprison us. If he had a cell already suited for storm dragons, then I highly doubted he would risk putting us anywhere else. Even if it meant revealing that Bexley's parents were alive, he'd probably consider it a win to ensure that none of us could escape. After all, if Bexley's parents —two of the most powerful shifters in Trabea— hadn't broken out in all these years, why would we?

The elevator jolted, and my brain misfired from the pain that shot through my body. My eyes squeezed shut for a mere moment, my brain dancing away from my fried nerve endings and presenting me with a far better memory...

My gaze followed Bexley as she waltzed through the Bronzehearts' gardens, making her way towards our spot. The spot where I always left notes to her. She didn't realize it, of course, but I'd chosen the spot because it was where we used to sit when we were kids and here to visit Gage. Where we used to sit for hours, talking and watching the world around us.

Where I unintentionally fell in love with her, even at such a young age.

This evening her golden hair was loose, hanging around her shoulders. The way her pale pink dress clung to her figure nearly made me groan and give myself away. I swear, the woman looked like candy. Constantly.

Rubbing a hand over my chest, I had to control the urge to go to her. To see the recognition in her gaze. To feel her in my arms.

But what if none of that happened? Or worse, what if it caused her an immense amount of pain? That possibility was more than enough to keep me in my place. My heart beat hard and loud for this woman, my pulse in time with her steps. If it meant waiting years for her to remember me, then that was exactly what I would sacrifice.

I smiled as Bexley picked up the note I'd hidden and immediately unfolded it. Her impatience was just one more thing I loved about her. Her beautiful face lit up as she read the note, and I savored each of her reactions from where I was crouched down, keeping out of sight.

As she flitted back toward the house, nearly dancing, I felt fulfilled knowing that I had made her happy, even if just momentarily.

"Breaker. We should leave if we don't want their security to see us." I nearly rolled my eyes at my own security officer's concern. Dennis was a good guy. Young but really good at his job, so I didn't give him too much shit—even now, when I knew that Gage was very well aware of my presence. He'd never begrudge my visits to check in on mo chuisle.

"Move. Now."

My eyes snapped open as I was shoved forward, out of the elevator. I quickly took in the new surroundings, attempting to orient and familiarize myself with the new environment—a darkened corridor—before searching out Bexley.

A small, wounded sound that had Linan scoffing escaped her throat. I reached out to her through our connection, needing to confirm that she was okay. The small residual piece left of our magic picked up on my will, a spark ignited along our mating bond.

"Breaker?" Bexley's sweet voice filled my chest with relief. She stood in front of me, surrounded by a black

glowing aura. Her golden eyes were filled with black stars where the white should have been, and her hands, which were clasping mine, were covered in scales. It was both beautiful and odd seeing her in this half-shifted state.

It was almost like it was her dragon there, communicating with me in the most human form it could manage.

"Are you okay? How are you feeling?" I demanded as she melted into me, her eyes filled with so much affection that it was damn near overwhelming.

When I brought my hand up to cup her cheek, I noticed that my own hand was covered in scales. They reflected in the dim light of the dreamscape, the flickering light making me think our collective subconscious was unable to create a more complicated landscape because of our drained power.

"Worried. I can't feel the others. Are they okay?"

"Unconscious, but okay. We've been transported to some sort of industrial complex. I'm hoping it's the same place where he's holding your parents." Bexley nodded in understanding, pressing her head against my chest, as I tried to catch the rumble that threatened to break out. I hated seeing fear on her face, even if it was for her mates' wellbeing. There should be no fear to begin with.

"He said something to me about ensuring Fletcher and I got to know each other better, even if it meant waiting till the next Black Moon. I'm worried about what he's going to try. We need to wake up, I just don't know how."

"I'm positive they'll be waking us up soon, whether we want to or not," I growled, unable to hide the rage at Linan's plan for my mate. Wrapping my arms around her, she melted into me, and a vow slipped from my lips before I could stop it. "I won't let him or anyone else touch you, Bex. Fletcher included."

Before she could respond, the world around us crumbled.

The metallic clang of the elevator doors closing behind us had reality filtering back in. A groan left my throat as I sat up and searched out my mate, only to find that I could barely see anything. At least not until my eyes adjusted.

We were in a cell of some kind, the faintest light from down the corridor illuminating the massive bars. A wavering wall of silver light—a ward, no doubt—moved between them. It was peaceful, almost, though I knew that peace would disappear if I tried to touch it. It would fucking hurt, for one, and it'd probably be enough to knock me unconscious considering my lack of power right now. Something I could also blame the damn wards for.

At least the stone floor was warm. It made me feel grounded and solid, unlike the walls which soared so high that I couldn't see the ceiling.

Apart from that, nothing else stood out to me. Except the obvious—*I was separated from Bexley*.

Looking around, I found Jagger slumped against the wall and Gage only a few feet away. But neither Bexley, Rachel, nor the Clanguard brothers were anywhere to be found. Moving sluggishly towards the front of the cell, I could feel both the physical effects of the power drain weighing on me heavily. They'd taken our bags and other personal belongings, luckily released our hands from cuffs, but my sphere was still in my jacket—hidden from sight, where it would stay until we decided to use it.

"Bexley?" I called out.

"She's over here." Fletcher's voice was filled with exhaustion. "She's here with us. Well, technically Thomas and Rachel are in the next cell over, but on this side of the corridor."

"Fuck," I growled. "Fletcher, I have no idea what your father is fucking thinking—what does he think this will accomplish? Doesn't he realize the clan leaders will immediately realize something went wrong?"

"He's *not* thinking," he groaned. "He's just being an egotistical bastard."

"Have you been down here before?" I asked, looking down the corridor. All I could see was a massive pair of dark doors, different than the elevator shaft doors. I couldn't feel any other magical signatures, but that probably meant jack shit down here.

"No, but I think this is where we want to be."

"Can't see shit down here," I growled.

"And there is no way we're going to be able to get out of these cells on our own."

"We have something that may work," I hinted, "but let's wait till the others wake up." Fletcher agreed, and I circled the cell before sitting down near the wall at the front of the cell, looking toward the doors at the other end of the hallway. The floor dipped in front of them, but I didn't know what that meant.

Frowning, I joined the others, propping myself up against the stone wall as I tried to get some rest. I didn't allow myself to get too comfortable, though. I wanted to be able to wake up immediately if someone joined us down here. Until then, I would try to reconnect with Bexley until she woke.

I expected a memory or dreamscape, but instead I was hit with a vision.

"Mommy!" A little voice pealed with laughter as I found Bexley once again in a garden, this time holding a small wrapped up bundle. A toddler, maybe around three years old, ran around her while giggling and tugging on her dress. The softness on Bexley's face, the true affection and love there, held me captive.

"Yes?" Bexley crouched down and adjusted the baby in her arms. The little girl leaned over and gave the baby a kiss on the nose, causing the child to stir. I assumed they wouldn't see me as I approached, but my feet on the gravel had both of them looking up.

"Daddy!" the girl exclaimed, launching herself at me. As I caught her, a well of emotion stirred. She was so overjoyed to simply see me.

Bexley's gaze was filled with a knowing light as she moved closer, her tone soft. "This is new. I've never had a dream like this before."

"Dream?" the little girl asked.

"Nothing, honey," Bexley promised. The little girl squirmed out of my arms and ran toward a pot of flowers on the stone patio, picking them up carefully and bringing them over. I had so many things I

wanted to say, but none of them seemed right. None were perfect enough to encapsulate how I felt.

The baby stirred, and when I looked down at his face, his eyes opened. I knew those eyes well—I saw them in the mirror every single day. One gold. One black.

"Bex. Open your eyes, cupcake." Gage's voice had my own eyes snapping open as the dream unfortunately broke. Looking around, I was able to see much better than I had before. There was a glowing light coming from Bexley's cell, Fletcher staring at her in unabashed surprise from several feet away. It was only then that I realized that *she* was the one surrounded by light.

She struggled to sit up, looking dazed, but when her gaze met mine, a small smile broke onto her face. *She remembered the dream.* I wanted to stay in that moment for just a little longer, but all too soon reality began to filter back in.

"He really did it," she whispered. "That's insane."

"What?" Jagger asked.

"Linan. He took us right to the place, the exact one from my dreams...but the power signature I usually sense is gone." Her gaze moved toward the doors at the end of the hall. "I don't want to consider why that is. Maybe it has to do with the wards or something."

I hadn't considered that he would have gotten rid of her parents before we arrived here. Surely not after this long, right? *Shit.*

"Being in the right place would be wonderful if there was even a chance of getting out. Which there isn't," Thomas pointed out, having finally woken up.

Before I could suggest the spheres, an unexpected voice chimed in. "I think I can help with that."

Chapter 9

Bexley Blackforge

Rebecca stepped out from the shadows, the silvery surface of our prison's wards warping my view of her. I could see her slight frame and the cloak she wore as she walked towards my cell, but her normally powerful aura was completely blocked.

I hadn't even known she was here until she spoke, which gave me hope that it was the wards blocking our ability to feel my parents' magic and not something worse.

Although I wouldn't have put it past Linan, especially if he thought his new prisoners were more valuable than my parents were. Plus, if they had their power drained and couldn't fight as they normally would...no. I wouldn't consider that.

I would get out and go through the doors at the

end of the hallway and figure it out myself. I refused to believe we'd done all of this for nothing.

"How did you get down here?" I asked, my voice betraying my shock.

"Who are you?" Fletcher demanded. He positioned himself between Rebecca and Rachel, even though Rachel was in the cell next to ours, thick iron bars separating us. I guess Linan thought that if we were physically separated from our mates then he could control us. If that was the case, he was dead wrong—both Fletcher and I were loyal to our mates, and there was absolutely nothing that would change that.

"I cloaked myself so that no one could see me and followed all of you down here. Even though we were traveling from different realms, I arrived at the portal only a few moments before you," she explained. "I don't have much power left, but I have enough to help. I only fear I won't be as useful when it comes to the war."

"Any little bit helps," Breaker countered.

"He's right," I agreed. "We're thankful you're here."

"We do have a potential problem." She looked between the three cages. "I'll be able to break down the wards on this side of the corridor, but I'm not sure I can do the other side—the magic they've imbued in each of these barriers…well, it's powerful. Some of the most powerful wards I've seen outside of Carmina. And the magic at the end of the hall is even more so. I fear that this entire effort may be in vain if I can only remove one side."

"We went to Carmina," I explained, pulling the small sphere Moloch created from my jacket. Rebecca watched me in surprise, coming closer to the cell but not so close that she touched the silvery wards. I could hear my mates moving around across the way, no doubt checking their spheres, and I was thrilled to see that despite us being knocked unconscious, transported to a prison, and placed in power-draining wards—the spheres were perfectly safe. Not only safe, but charged up. At least mine was.

"Did yours get charged from the portal?" I called out, rolling the sphere between my fingers. The orb was silver and felt hot to the touch, like a white-hot fire was burning inside.

"Mine doesn't seem as bright as the other two, but yes," Jagger answered as the others said something that I didn't fully catch. There was tension in his voice, and I knew a large part of it had to do with us being separated so soon after solidifying our mate bond.

Honestly, I wished all three of my mates had been part of the dream I shared with Breaker, if only to give them solace that we'd make it through this okay. The experience of a vision like that was like none other, and I planned on telling them about it as soon as I could. Maybe it would serve as a beacon of comfort in the absolute chaotic mess we now found ourselves in.

"Who made these?" Rebecca asked.

"An associate of the Nyx family," Gage answered.

She nodded as if that explained everything. "If that's the case, you may be able to use them from within the cell to break open the ward."

"We need our power to trigger them, and these wards, unfortunately, are draining our power as we speak," Jagger grunted. My brow dipped in concern. I hated the idea of them undergoing any power drain, let alone one of this magnitude.

"Of course," Rebecca murmured, studying the object a moment longer, her brows furrowed before she met my gaze once more. "That's a dangerous object you're holding, but it'll serve our purposes once you have your power back. First things first, though—let's get this ward down."

Before I had a chance to ask her how she planned on doing that, she dropped her hood and pushed up the sleeves of her robe, revealing her scaled and clawed hands.

I jumped in surprise as she suddenly slammed her hand against the ward, the violent action taking me off guard. At first nothing happened, but her confidence didn't waver. With the slowest movement in the world, she pierced the ward with her claw and whispered a singular foreign word under her breath. I immediately felt the air shift, a wave of dizziness nearly overtaking me with the amount of magic sizzling around us.

Slowly at first, stems of black ivy grew out of her palms, thickening into branches as they began to climb the ward aggressively. I stepped back to watch them climb higher and higher until they reached the top, where I could no longer see them in the darkness of the room.

Then...*it broke.*

All at once the ward shattered, icy blue shards of magic crashing to the floor. I instinctively shielded my head, but the shards faded into nothing, disappearing as if they'd never truly existed in the first place. I watched with bated breath as Rebecca ran her hand between the prison bars and met no resistance.

Before I could take a step forward, a body darted in front of me, Fletcher rushing from our cell to pull Thomas and Rachel out of theirs. I smiled at their reunion before looking towards my own mates.

Walking up to the ward, I stared at my three men in concern. Breaker offered me a smile that was far too relaxed for the moment—and one I didn't buy for a second—but I could feel their relief that I was no longer in that cell. Rebecca walked up to me, standing by my side as she adjusted her robe and looked at the ward with disdain. Shattering the other one had visibly taken a lot out of her, and I worried that she wouldn't be able to do it again. That I'd be forced to find Linan and somehow make him release my mates.

"This one will take longer," Rebecca said as she fortified herself for another round, the determined gaze in her eye making me feel hopeful that she'd be able to do it.

"That's fine, we can keep a watch out," Fletcher said, nodding towards the elevators. I shifted on my feet, desperately wanting to reach out to my mates.

"Go to your parents, Bexley. Use your orb to blast that damn lock. We won't waste it on this ward when I should be able to handle it—I have a feeling you'll need all the firepower you have when it's time to release your parents. The one you have should take care of the ward externally and hopefully release the power drain on your parents...unless he has another one on the inside. We'll follow shortly after just in case since your mates have three more orbs.

"Your parents will be very weak, and they may not recognize you," Rebecca warned as a second thought. "Don't fear them. They won't hurt you once they realize who you are."

Which meant that I had to hope they would recognize me, and fast.

"Don't go alone!" Gage's words came out all in a rush, and for once he let his worry show outwardly, not bothering to school his expression for anyone else.

"Or wait for us," Jagger rumbled, his gaze narrowing on Rebecca as if she were purposefully putting me in danger. I knew that wasn't the case, though, and we needed to speed up this process in case Linan came back. Still, I couldn't blame them for worrying. This could go terribly wrong.

Glancing nervously between the doors at the end of the hall and my mates, I said, "I love you guys, and I understand why you're concerned...but I need to do this. By myself."

Without another word, and before I could second-guess my decision, I walked past the empty cells that lined both sides of the hall. The space was saturated with magic, the wards having hidden it from us before, and I could feel when Rebecca started working on my mates' cell. Swallowing nervously, I approached the double doors that had played a starring role in my recent dreams.

If I was right, my parents would be right behind them.

"You've got this," I murmured to myself as I placed my orb on the lock. When I stepped back, though, I realized I had a problem.

My own power had been drained, and I wasn't sure how I was going to trigger the thing. Frowning, I closed my eyes and searched for the flame inside of me.

After what felt like minutes I finally found it, the flame diminished to a glowing ember. It was trying to grow with minimal success. Inhaling sharply, I pulled on it, sweat beading on the back of my neck as I brought my hands together, cupping them and willing my magic to pool inside.

Wind brushed over me, tickling my arms, and above me the sky seemed to rumble despite being inside. It was a shadow of my normal magic, but I soon realized it was growing and that my mates were feeding it—our bonds lit up as they willingly shared their magic. Tears of gratitude welled in my eyes as I pushed for more.

Black electricity suddenly jumped between my

fingers, my eyes snapping open as a bolt struck the lock. *Hard.*

I stumbled back as the sphere detonated, heat brushing over my face as I raised my arm to shield it. My skin stung from the burn, but the pain—a mere echo of what I'd felt when attacked by the electricity of the taser—was completely overshadowed by the realization that the door was *open.*

Smoke curled out the cell, and I crept towards it, cautious. The darkness that lay before me felt eternal, but I wasn't scared. Not exactly.

How could I be when I recognized the energy inside?

There was no doubt about it: my parents were in there.

Turning around, I felt relief at seeing that Rebecca's black vines were halfway up the other warded wall. I had no idea what Linan could or couldn't hear; could or couldn't sense from above. I had no idea if he had cameras, but it didn't matter because my men were nearly out and my parents were feet away. Deciding to be as brave as my men, I slipped through the door. The moment my feet touched the stone on the other side, golden flames erupted around me.

It wasn't enough to help me see through the

pitch black of the room, but it did make me feel better...*until the door behind me slammed shut.*

"Shit!" I gasped, my adrenaline surging as the flames died out.

Standing there in the void of darkness, I closed my eyes and pulled on my power, a subtle glow surrounding me once more. My heartbeat was loud, and the light flickered along with it. My magic was returning slowly, and it felt like a constant struggle to maintain it. Like I was barely treading water. I hated the feeling.

"Hello? Mom? Dad?" It felt foreign saying those words, but it did help dispel the fear. Maybe, *just maybe,* they wouldn't view me as a threat. All I could do was hope, because the reality was that they hadn't seen me in eight years, and they'd certainly only known enemies in this place. My brain still struggled with the fact that they were alive after all this time; the concept seemed too good to be true. So I'm sure that for them, the thought of seeing me was likely the same.

As I stepped further into the room, a faint glow began to grow opposite of me. Or at least I thought that was the case...until I realized it was another ward reflecting my own glow. This ward, though, felt more like a vacuum. Like it had enough power to just siphon and siphon without restraint. I was going to need my mates and their spheres for sure.

Stepping closer, my hand reached up and I considered touching it—

A scream caught in my throat as I nearly fell back onto the stone floor.

A face, stark and gaunt, appeared on the other side, wide eyes staring at me with a furious, hateful expression. *Holy crap.* Holding my heart, I took a moment to catch my breath as the woman pounded against the ward, sparks flying around her. If it hurt her, she didn't act like it, and the way her hair flew around her made her look like she was surrounded by flames.

It was only then, my stomach dipping, that I realized who I was looking at: my mom.

Her frame was smaller than it had been in my visions, her dark clothes hanging off of her. Any life or glow to her skin was completely absent. Somehow I could feel the imprint of her magic, an echo of what it once was, and my own reached out to her. Her eyes were manic, though, filled with an intensity and aggression that scared me. She was intimidating, even in this state.

"Mom?" My voice cracked as her gaze narrowed on me, her fist pounding the ward once more.

Walking forward, I spoke more clearly. "It's me. Bexley. Your daughter."

Her face grew impossibly angrier as she let out a predatory hiss. "I know who you are. You've come to me again and again in dreams, a cruel vision at most!"

"No!" I squeaked, horrified. "I'm here. Really."

"Impossible," she growled.

Looking at the ward that separated us, I decided to do something that I'd probably regret. I crossed through the ward and into the other side, not knowing if I'd ever be able to get out.

Chapter 10

Bexley Blackforge

The minute I crossed through the ward, my back was slammed back against it. Somehow it'd become as solid as cement in a fraction of a second.

Two hands grasped my shoulders, pushing as if they could shove me back through. An enraged sound came from my mother as we locked gazes, her next demand echoing through the darkened room. "What are you doing?!"

A horrified expression broke out onto her face as her touch suddenly disappeared, my mom moving away quickly as if burned. Her sudden departure caused me to stumble slightly before straightening myself up. Offering her a bewildered look, I put my hands out. "What do you mean 'what am I doing'? I'm proving that I'm actually here!"

And *here* was very different than the other side.

Despite the darkness and the shadows that moved like they were alive, I could make out faint shapes. Furniture, possibly. There was also the dripping sound of water somewhere in the background. One spot directly behind my mom was particularly dark, and I could feel magic radiating from that direction. It was faint, but I had a feeling that it was my dad...so why wasn't he out here with her?

"I *hope* this is a dream and that you aren't here! Are you out of your mind?"

Her words hit me like a slap. I winced, leaning against the ward and wrapping my arms around myself protectively. "What do you mean? Why wouldn't you want me here? I'm here to get you out."

I mean, why else had they continued to appear in my dreams? I had to assume it was because they were reaching out for help, because *they wanted to get out*...right? Or had my knowledge of them brought forth the dreams?

"There *is* no out! And if you're really here, now you're stuck too!"

Tears welled in my eyes. It felt like she was rejecting me. I understood rationally that she wasn't, but after finding out that they were still alive, after remembering my childhood...

This hadn't been how I had imagined our reunion.

I thought she'd want to see me again, this woman who gave birth to me. Who had loved me so much that she'd put an elaborate plan into motion to keep me safe from those in the realm who wanted to hurt me.

We were finally together, and instead of celebrating that...well, I had no idea what we were doing.

"At least we're together again." My voice was weak, dejected. But my words must have finally struck home because all the anger in her expression just...disappeared.

For a long moment, my mom went completely and utterly still, staring at me in shock. No...not staring, but truly *looking*—examining me head to toe. That was when I saw the change happen; when realization hit her. When her eyes began to fill with tears, her lips tightening as she tried to keep them from turning down.

This time when she slammed into me, it wasn't violent. It was a hug. Possibly the tightest hug I'd ever received, her frail arms so unyielding it was almost painful. Her body shook with sobs, and the sound of her cries echoing through the void of the chamber had tears streaming down my own cheeks.

So many emotions fought for dominance—happiness to be with her again, worry for her wellbeing, fear that I'd ruined our chances of escaping—but the relief that she'd remembered me, that she believed I was here to help her, and just that she was here, alive, and it wasn't some cruel joke...those were the feelings that won out. I was with my mom! *My actual mom.*

Our magics, though practically nonexistent behind the ward, reached out to one another and collided. A flash of light filled the space, surrounding us in flames. My eyes fluttered shut as memories began to play behind my eyelids, images flashing by in rapid succession. Not just my memories, though, but *hers.* Somehow I was experiencing, feeling, and seeing my mom's memories.

Of the day I was born and when she held me for the first time.

Of watching me walk towards my dad on unsteady legs.

Of when I shifted and flew for the first time.

Hot tears streamed down my cheeks as a part of myself, the one that harbored the little girl who was still wounded from being abandoned in an alley, was healed. I could feel her love for me. I could feel through her memories how much both of my parents loved me. While I had known for several days that they were possibly still alive, I don't think I'd truly believed that they were...or that if they were alive, they could want me after all of this time—at least not until now.

"Bexley." My mom pulled back, relief and joy clear on her face. "My goodness, you have grown up so much—you're beautiful, honey, and so powerful. I had no idea—*no idea* that those dreams would actually lead you here. I thought that I'd...well, I'd imagined so many times what you would be like as an adult, and I assumed it was a simple dream."

"I had no idea you were still alive until I found Rebecca."

"Found her?" she asked, looking alarmed.

"I have so much to tell you about what's happened," I said, squeezing her hands, "but I'm just so happy to be here with you."

"We'll have a lot of time to talk," she agreed softly, needing to convince herself as much as me. "I don't know how we'll manage to get out of here; I wish I hadn't forced your hand. Then you could have at least stayed on the other side."

"Please don't worry. I'm not here alone. My friends, Rebecca, and my mates—"

"Mates?" Her gaze lit with warm excitement. "You mean Gage, Jagger, and Breaker are here? I'm so glad you were reunited with them, that Rebecca was able to eventually bring you back to them."

"That didn't happen...not exactly." I ran a hand

through my hair as I shifted on my feet, not wanting her to be mad at Rebecca for not sticking to the plan. "As Rebecca was planning to leave with me, Clanguard's men attacked us. She put a memory spell on me and transported me to the middle of the city, as far away as possible. The Bronzehearts found me, and she managed to escape and hide in Natura."

My voice softened, thick with sadness as I finished my explanation. "I had no memories of my childhood; no knowledge of who I was. I thought the Bronzehearts had taken me in out of kindness, because the memory spell triggered immense pain when they tried to tell me anything else."

My mom was speechless, her face a mask of shock, so I continued, wanting to move past it. "It's okay, though—they took really good care of me. And when I turned eighteen and went to DIA, it all started coming back, and my mates were right there to help me process all of it."

Even I had to admit that was possibly shortening the story slightly, but I felt overwhelmed by the amount of information she needed to know paired with the intensity of emotions I felt. "But like you said, we have plenty of time. I can explain more later. To answer your question, though, yes, the three of them are here. How...how did you know they were my mates?"

Inhaling, she seemed to shake herself before offering a small shrug. "I suppose I didn't fully know, but it always seemed obvious to me. They were attached to you from the moment you met. The other moms and I always entertained the possibility..." She trailed off, caught in her thoughts, sadness filling her expression.

"They're all safe, I promise. I also promise that I'll explain how we got here once we escape. The others should be here soon, so we're going to need to leave fast. Where's Dad?" I'd been alert for any sign of his presence as I'd talked to Mom, but I never got anything more concrete than my initial feeling that he was here somewhere.

My mom tensed and squeezed her eyes shut, running a hand over her chest as if my question caused her physical pain. She looked towards what I could now see was a pitch-black hallway leading further back. My eyes had adjusted to the darkness the longer I stared into it, and that allowed me to see their meager belongings. Linan had given them absolutely nothing all of these years, and I hated him for it. I also couldn't for the life of me figure out how they'd survived in this place for so long...I mean, what had they even eaten? I would have to ask, but now wasn't the time.

"He's in the back, sleeping—well, unconscious.

This sleep has lasted a lot longer than the others... I can still feel his dragon, though, and our mate bond. He's okay for now." The words she left unsaid spoke volumes—he may not be okay for much longer.

"I don't understand." I frowned as I stepped toward the dark hall, my mom right by my side. "Why is he in such worse shape than you?"

"He's been feeding me magic from the start," she said in long-suffering resignation. "Your dad wanted me to be as strong as possible in case *he* tried anything again. I told him to stop time and time again, but the man has always been stubborn."

I stopped hard. "In case who tried anything?" I already had an idea, but I needed confirmation.

"Linan," she bit out. "When he first took us captive, he tried to force me to mate with him, but your dad always protected me. I'm positive he has a witch on his side—although I've never seen them— who specializes in power drainage. That's where the wards come from—where most of Linan's power comes from. The witch drains the power from our dragons. And your father, even though he's nearly completely drained himself, is giving me magic. It's insane, but no matter how many times I implore him to stop, he won't."

"Linan is trying to mate me to his son," I said, and my mom's eyes flared. "I hate him."

"When we leave here, I will kill him," she vowed.

I squeezed her arm. "There may be a few people willing to fight you for the privilege." Like my mates. Although if anyone truly deserved the honor, it was her—he'd taken everything from her, and he was still threatening to do so now.

"Let's see your dad," she whispered, leading me forward.

"Has Linan been down here recently?" I asked. As we walked through the rough walls of the tunnel, I realized it was possible my parents had dug these tunnels on their own. Maybe the tunnel was their eventual escape plan.

"No, unless he visited and we weren't aware, which is unlikely. I haven't seen the bastard in five years or so."

"How have you survived? How'd you get food and water?"

"We didn't. I think he expected for us to starve and die. What he doesn't realize is that there are only a few ways to truly kill a dragon, and starvation isn't one of them. We aren't weak like the wolves. We aren't so easily disposed of." The venom in her voice eased as she added, "It's not helping your father's condition, though."

"The minute we get out, we'll get you anything and everything you need," I promised her. I did wonder what could kill a dragon considering he'd managed to slaughter those in the Flash clan, but that was a conversation for a different time.

Her eyes filled with warmth. "I don't need much, just your father and you. But I'm glad you were taken care of and that Celine found you. She was good to you?"

"Amazing, Mom. And when she told me about you two after the memory spell broke, she told me she never wanted to replace you but to do right by you."

My mom squeezed my hand, her eyes warming with affection. "That's sweet of her, and it doesn't surprise me. Celine was always thinking about others. With that being said, I understand if she feels more like a mother to you than I do."

"No. You're my mom. She's amazing, literally like a second mom. But once my memories of my childhood returned, I understood why I felt so much grief all these years. I didn't know why I was in mourning for two people who I thought had abandoned me, but now I realize it was because some part of me thought you were dead. The memory spell wiped *everything*, but even it couldn't wipe away my love."

My mom's words were soft as she squeezed my hand once more, "Your father and I have always loved you. Clanguard would have loved to erase our memories, erase the truth we knew, but he could never. Our love for you surpasses his power."

We stepped into a dimly lit room at the end of her statement, torches lining the walls. The cozy space was more like a bedroom, and my eyes widened at the large but thin frame laid out on the bed. *My dad.*

He was easily over 6'5", and I knew from my memories that he'd once been intimidating, the set of his shoulders wide and formidable, but his body was now a skeletal husk of its former self.

Grabbing his hand and wrapping it in both of mine to try and warm his cold fingers, I spoke in a soft voice. "Hey Dad. I don't know if you can hear me, but it's Bex. I'm here to rescue you and Mom. You're finally going to get out of here."

My mom sniffled behind me, wiping tears away with the back of her hand.

"When the others come and break the ward, the guys may need to carry him out," I warned her after evaluating his state. My brow dipped in thought. "There is one thing I still can't figure out—one thing that's bothering me."

"What's that?" she asked, adjusting one of the torches so I could see my dad's face better.

"Why would Linan put us down here?"

My mom stilled. "I'm not sure. I guess it doesn't make much sense, when you think about it."

"Maybe he *wanted* me to get in here and try to break you guys out. Didn't you say that Dad has been blocking him from getting to you from the start?"

"But then he'd have had to know that you had the ability to break out yourself and then us," she pointed out. "He hasn't come down here in nearly half a decade, so I'm not sure why he would choose to release us now—after all, he'd always been able to go in and out through the main door in those first three years. Honestly, I'm surprised they were able to capture the four of you in the first place, I doubt he would create an entire plan based around the ability to do that."

It did feel almost embarrassing that we'd been taken prisoner, but the way she said it was without judgment.

"We were coming back through a portal, completely caught us off guard. I mean, I'm glad it brought us down here, but we probably should've predicted that. I just don't understand why he'd risk putting us here without leaving any guards on the off chance we could break out."

"He probably didn't think anything of it," she murmured, shaking her head with an expression of disgust. "Clanguard's pride and ego are his downfall."

I looked back down at my dad in thought. "I'm going to give him a little bit of magic, enough to wake him up."

"You don't have to do that, Bexley."

"I do," I whispered. Even though my magic was nearly depleted, I could still attempt to do some good. Closing my eyes, I pushed magic towards him, my hand resting on top of his. Waves of heat broke off of me like flames, gently licking over his cold skin.

There was an immediate reaction when our magics connected. With my mom there had been so many memories and emotions, but with my dad it was different. It was possibly because of his state of mind, being so close to death, but only a singular memory came across. A powerful one that said *everything* in a singular second.

It was my dad holding me for the first time, one hand wrapped around me and the other holding my mom's hand. The medical center bustled around them, but a peaceful cloud of joy was wrapped around the three of us. I could feel everything he'd felt in that moment and everything he continued to feel. The intensity of his loyalty and love towards our family.

It was what he was still living for. That singular

memory was keeping his foot in this world, instead of giving into the void. I sniffed, trying to not break out into fresh tears, as I opened my eyes to look down at my dad's face, feeling his fingers squeeze weakly around my own.

"Bexley." His whisper of my name was echoed by a clap of thunder as I heard the doors slam open.

My mates were here.

Chapter 11

Jagger Silvershade

As we walked through the doors of the room Bexley had disappeared into, the stone around our feet lit up into flames, revealing a towering ward and absolutely no Bexley in sight. Pulling on our connection, I immediately realized what had happened.

"She went through the ward," Gage guessed.

"I won't be able to bring those down," Rebecca admitted, standing on the other side of the door we'd just blasted open again. Not because the ward and lock had reappeared—the orb Bexley used had taken care of that— but because there had been some other type of magical trap in place. One that made the doors slam shut and impossible to open from the inside, my gaze running over the lack of handles in the interior.

As a precaution, Thomas, Fletcher, and Rachel were standing outside on watch with Rebecca nearby, just in case. It was my hope that if we did get trapped in here, they'd be able to figure out how to open the doors once more with the aid of her somewhat depleted magic. Hoping that we didn't have to utilize that option, I recognized we needed to figure out where the hell Bexley had gone and why she'd chosen to go through the ward in the first place.

"So we need to bring them down, then. Everyone back up," I called out. I placed my sphere down at the base of the warded wall and retreated along with Gage and Breaker, allowing my power to dance between my fingertips. Above us, the unending ceiling seemed to grow cloudy as lightning flashed, creating a pseudo-storm within the chamber.

A phantom wind picked up, and once I felt like I'd amassed enough power—something that took quite a bit longer than usual—I threw my hand up and blasted it toward the sphere. I probably should've given a warning, but the big clap of thunder right at the moment of collision served as announcement enough.

The resulting explosion was powerful enough that it sent me flying back into the stone wall of the doors, my head slamming against the hard surface.

Blood dripped into my eye from a cut made by a piece of debris that had shot up from the floor. My head pounded and my vision was literally tinged red, but those were only minor annoyances compared to the realization that it had all been for *nothing*.

The sphere had created the smallest crack in the ward, but it wasn't growing.

"Again."

"Wait!" Before I could finish my directive, Bexley appeared on the other side of the ward. "That won't work. One won't work. You need at least two at the same time."

Thank the fates I had eyes on her once more, although her image seemed muted and fuzzy. I couldn't see exactly how she was doing, and that didn't sit right with me.

She turned as if someone said something behind her before looking back at us, her eyes filled with a thrum of excitement I could feel through our bond. She must have found her parents—that was the only explanation.

"We only have two left. If this doesn't work, we have no more options," Gage said. "I know Moloch told us to use them from fifty feet away, but we won't be able to in here. We ignored his advice just now, and now Jagger is bleeding. He also mentioned not using more than one, and I don't want to risk losing both of our orbs as well as possibly hurting you in the process."

"I promise you we will be fine behind here," she insisted, the 'we' catching my attention and confirming my suspicions. "Just focus on doing both of them at the same time—I'm guessing it'll take all three of you. I have no magic behind this ward or else I'd try to help."

"It should work," Rebecca said, agreeing with Bex's plan. "You boys may just need to combine your powers, similar to how you would in battle." How was she even aware we could do that? Then again, our fathers had been the ones to teach us that, so it wasn't terribly surprising that she would be aware of it.

"I can call it," I said. We were connected enough that I'd be able to feel when we had enough power.

Breaker brought his and Gage's spheres up to the wall as Bexley backed away, out of sight. Then the three of us spaced ourselves out so that when we did use our magic, we could aim it at the precise point on the ward where the two spheres lay on the ground. Thunder rumbled overhead, and I hesitated when I considered the amount of power we were about to use. What if it broke through the barrier and hit our mate? No. If that had been possible, her parents would have done it long ago.

This plan would work—it had to work.

"Go!" I roared once the three of us had amassed enough power.

All at once, we released our magic to trigger the spheres and destroy the ward. I'd thought I'd seen the extent of the sphere's explosive power, but what happened next felt like we hadn't doubled its effect, but rather quadrupled it.

Electricity jumped between us and the ward, holding us in place as the wall behind us broke apart from the force of the explosion. The ceiling began to shake, and heavy pieces plunged to the ground. The doors fell with a heavy *thunk,* the ward shattering with the ear-piercing sound of nails on a chalkboard.

It had worked—it had fucking worked!

My magic retracted, and I stumbled slightly before catching myself and surging forward to find Bexley. Her back was against a cave wall, and her face and skin were covered in dirt, her clothes torn and burned.

I didn't bother holding back. Picking Bexley up in my arms, I tucked her against me and began to feed her magic, worried how low hers seemed to be. She was so drained, yet she was sharing what little she had with two others.

Two others who *weren't* my brothers.

Behind her, from inside the cave, movement had a rumble breaking from my throat.

"It's okay," Bexley said. "It's my parents."

I couldn't do anything but stare at my mate and blink stupidly. Of course finding her parents had been the goal of this entire trip to begin with, but a big part of me had been prepared for disappointment. For the possibility that they would either be dead or...well, altered in a way that meant they would never recover. That they had been subjected to so much trauma that the world outside of this prison, including Bexley, would be completely unrecognizable.

"Shit." Breaker darted forward to help as Mrs. Blackforge appeared, her frail arms wrapped around her husband who was somehow in even worse condition. Fuck. They had to be underweight by at least fifty pounds, and they clearly hadn't seen the sun for years, their skin so pale it was almost translucent. This was so fucked up.

If I hadn't hated Linan before, I definitely did now. Mr. and Mrs. Blackforge had always been pillars of the community, revered leaders of the land, so to see them like this...

I tightened my arms around Bexley, needing to know she was safe. That Clanguard hadn't been successful in imprisoning her as well.

"Let us help," Breaker said as he ducked under Mr. Blackforge's arm to shoulder his weight, Gage offering Mrs. Blackforge an elbow to step over the debris.

"Thank you," Mr. Blackforge said. "All of you."

"Absolutely," I said sincerely. "Let's get out of here so we can properly celebrate escaping. I worry our explosion will have drawn some attention."

"He absolutely heard that," Gage agreed. "How fast are the two of you able to travel? Would it help if we carried both of you?"

"No." Mrs. Blackforge straightened and held her husband's gaze, some type of communication passing between them. "We've lasted this long, and I want to walk out of here on my own. I won't leave frail and broken."

"Of course," Bexley said. I set her down on her feet, seeing she wanted to join her mom.

"Tell me, how did he bring you down here?"

"Freight elevator," Breaker answered. I cursed the fact that we hadn't been conscious for our arrival. While I felt like I had a decent grasp on the area around us now, I worried we'd be at a disadvantage once we got aboveground.

Earlier, when I'd been hit with bolts of electricity from the taser, I'd truly thought I'd died. I'd been mid-shift, needing to reach my mate, to protect her. Watching her convulse on the ground was agony, a living nightmare, and I couldn't have stopped my dragon if I'd wanted to. But when the bolt caught me in my half-shifted state, momentarily freezing me there, I felt as though I'd been split in half.

The magic had rebounded and turned me back human, but I'd lost consciousness immediately after, unable to handle what the shock had done to my system. And when I finally woke up and Bexley wasn't right next to me, I'd only been able to assume the worst. That he had taken her—imprisoned her.

I'd been right, too—he'd imprisoned all of us.

"We have a clear path right now," Fletcher said, urging us forward. Bexley's parents tensed, not having noticed the Clanguard brothers until now.

"They've turned on him," I assured them. "Allies. I promise."

Bexley nodded in confirmation, and they both relaxed. They'd been gearing up for a fight, even if they wouldn't have been able to help much, if at all. It shouldn't have surprised me; I'd always known them to be fearless.

"Rebecca?!" Mrs. Blackforge's voice broke as she strode past us, a new vigor to her step as she met Rebecca in the middle of the hall, the two of them embracing. Bexley let out a happy sound at the interaction, and I wrapped my arm around her shoulders. I wanted to talk to her about how she felt because I couldn't imagine that anything about this was emotionally easy, let alone the physical distress and injury she was suffering—an element that was affecting me as well.

As the rest of us approached the two women, Mr. Blackforge gave a weak smile. "Good to see you, Rebecca."

"You as well, Jericho. Your signature kept fading; I feared the worst."

"Can't get rid of me that easily." He chuckled. "I still have to beat you in chess."

"Never."

Mrs. Blackforge rolled her eyes. Bexley's gaze darted back and forth with interest, a smile playing on her lips.

"I hate to interrupt," Thomas interjected, "but we need to get moving."

"It isn't only us here," Mrs. Blackforge said, her expression solemn. "I can tell there are others—their power's been accumulating over the years. I fear Linan has been imprisoning more people, and the strongest signature is one that is several floors up from here."

"We have to help them," Bexley said immediately. "It wouldn't surprise me if he's holding others captive. I'm already convinced that many of his soldiers aren't fighting willingly."

"We don't have time to help them," Fletcher said, causing my face to twist into a look of distaste. I understood that he was worried about us getting out of here, but I very much stood on the same page as my mate.

Rachel stared at him in confusion as Bexley frowned, shaking her head. "We need to say something at least—even if it's just a promise to return. I will not leave without giving them some hope."

And I wasn't going to try to talk her out of trying to save women from this hell hole.

"Fine." Fletcher was stressed—we could all hear it in his voice—but he managed to keep it together as Mrs. Blackforge led us to a corridor near the elevators. Gage and Breaker began to explain to Bexley's parents how we'd gotten here, Rebecca chiming in about her part. As we stood in front of the elevator, my hand hesitating over the button to call it, I looked around, trying to seek out another method of escape.

"What's wrong?" Thomas asked.

"Linan will be waiting for us to use the elevator.

If there's another way to get out of here, we should try to find it."

"The elevator wasn't here when we arrived," Mrs. Blackforge noted. "They may have sealed it up by now, but we took a staircase down here."

Almost immediately, Gage was jogging over to a darkened corner of the hall. When he reemerged, his face was marred with concern. "There are stairs, but they are steep and go up farther than I can see."

"Jagger is right, Linan will be waiting for us," Mr. Blackforge got out roughly. "We should take the stairs."

No one argued. He was the one in the worst shape of all of us, so if he thought the stairs were the better choice, we weren't in any position to disagree.

We began to climb the stone staircase which winded up and up, our voices echoing in the narrow space. I felt claustrophobic but didn't say a word as we began our ascent, the smooth windowless and doorless walls seeming to repeat themselves again and again. How long had we been walking up the stairs at this point?

Finally, the anxiety-inducing monotony was broken. A red door sat to the side of the staircase, and Breaker didn't hesitate to open it. I gently led Bexley through ahead of me, wanting to keep her close in case we encountered any danger.

If we did, I would get her out of here before she could blink, especially now that we had a clear path upwards. Down below I still couldn't hear anything, so we had a bit of time—Clanguard apparently hadn't yet caught on that something was going on down here.

Still, I didn't want to test our luck for too long.

Mr. and Mrs. Blackforge, along with Gage and Rebecca, stayed outside the door so we didn't get locked in, but the rest of us continued inside. There were no wards covering these cells, and they were all empty...except one. At the far end was a gold-gilded cell that was dark inside, the slightest movement the only thing that made me think that someone was in there.

"Mom?" Thomas's voice was etched with pain as I watched a woman approach the bars from the shadows. I could see the resemblance. This was the woman that I'd met as a child, the one that Linan always treated like shit. Fletcher and Rachel moved past us as Bexley and I stayed rooted to the spot with Breaker.

"Didn't you say..." Rachel began.

"That we haven't been allowed to see her for years? Yes." Fletcher said, clenching his teeth in an obvious effort to rein in his emotions.

The woman flinched but kept an otherwise

neutral expression. "How long have you been here? When did he lock you up?"

"Years," she answered in a murmur. "This isn't my first cage."

"We have to get you out," Thomas said, frantically searching in the dark. "We have to find a key—"

"No. There are floors full of other women here. For years, he's been using the mates and children of his soldiers as leverage to ensure they would do his bidding. I can't leave, not until I know they're safe. More so, if he finds I've escaped...trust me, they'll be the ones to suffer for it." Her gaze moved past us as Mrs. Blackforge approached. "Ashley, I am so incredibly sorry for what he did—"

"Do not apologize, Carol," Mrs. Blackforge insisted. "His sins are his own. We can help you get out though."

"I vowed I would not leave these packlands until they are released. You should go. Regain your strength and come back for us. Please."

I didn't fully agree with her analysis, but I could tell that she probably wouldn't change her mind. We were nearly ready to leave when a rustling that sounded from behind her had all of us peering into the darkness.

"Mommy?"

Horror filled the Clanguard brothers' faces as a

little girl, maybe five, who looked just like them, moved toward their mom. Her eyes were an odd, milky texture, and it made me wonder if she'd ever been outside—somehow I thought not. Linan didn't seem the type to do something so 'generous.'

"Who—who is that?" Fletcher demanded.

Their mother's face was drawn as she explained. "Your sister. She was born right after I disappeared. Or whatever story your father told everyone. He was embarrassed to have a girl—said it made him weak."

"But I'm not weak," the little girl said proudly. Bexley moved out of my arms and to Rachel's side, the two of them crouching down to look at the girl. She was small enough to fit through the bars, meaning that she chose her imprisonment so she could stay with her mom. She probably didn't even know there was another choice.

I'd already known it, but the sight of the little girl drove the point home—Linan was a vile individual, a creature who didn't deserve to be called a 'person.' When such a creature hurt others, it was despicable. But when it hurt the vulnerable, like children, the worst—and final—punishment was called for. One I'd be thrilled to administer.

"What a piece of shit," Breaker murmured.

"We had no idea. We thought..."

"Your dad's a bastard," Carol said, "but we can

talk about that later. You need to leave now. They're going to search each floor for you if you've escaped from downstairs—I'm assuming that explosion was you? I'm surprised the place didn't collapse."

Bexley snapped her head up, panicked at the thought. I fought the urge to go and comfort her, opting instead to send soothing waves down our bond so that I didn't interrupt the conversation she and Rachel were having with the girl. This place wasn't going to collapse anytime soon; it's why it was perfect for holding so many.

"No," Fletcher said, unyielding. "We're not leaving without you."

"I said go," she hissed. When neither Thomas nor Fletcher budged, Carol chose a different tactic, turning to Rachel. "You're their mate? The one Linan told me about?"

Rachel hesitated. "He mentioned me?"

"Yes. He hates you—which made me like you a lot more."

The statement made Mrs. Blackforge laugh as Bexley nodded in agreement.

"Yes. I'm Rachel."

"I wish we were meeting under better circumstances, but I need to ask something of you," Carol said earnestly. "Take Olivia with you. Keep her safe.

I don't want him to use her against me when the war starts."

Shit.

"Of course," Rachel said, not even hesitating.

"Don't underestimate Linan," Carol said, addressing all of us now. "Take care of my baby girl."

"Mommy, I don't want to leave," the little girl cried.

"No, no," Rachel soothed. "It will be fun, I promise."

"Go with Rachel and Bex, Olivia. They'll take care of you and keep you safe until I can join you. I'll be right behind you, okay? I love you." Pressing a kiss to Olivia's forehead, Carol gently pushed her through the bars to Rachel, who scooped her up and strode straight out the door without a backwards glance. Bex, Breaker, and I left Fletcher and Thomas to say their parting words, continuing our journey up the stairs. It was a hell of a long way up, and it felt like an eternity before we reached the metal door at the top.

Bexley pushed through it, the sunlight blinding after having spent so many hours in the dark. Bex's parents and Olivia shielded their eyes, and we paused to give them time to acclimate. They still couldn't open their eyes and needed assistance to move, but *we'd made it*. We'd broken free and released her parents.

Bexley squeezed my hand and I strode forward, more determined than ever to get out of here. We would come back, and we would free every single person here—no one would remain under Clanguard's thumb. The bastard's reign was over, and when we were done there wouldn't be a single piece left of him.

Chapter 12

Bexley Blackforge

My brow dipped in confusion as I looked around the roof we stood on, trying to figure out when we'd broken the surface while traveling up the winding staircase from underground. I hadn't felt any temperature or pressure difference, nor had there been any windows to signal it. It was disorienting, and I wasn't sure how we were going to handle our current predicament.

Not all of us could shift into an animal that flies, and even among those of us who could, we weren't in the best shape. But there wasn't another easy way to get down without going back down the staircase, which was an option I wanted to avoid. Aside from the fact that we'd heard the footsteps of Linan's men down below on the last leg of our journey, I doubted I'd be able to restrain myself a second time from checking each and every floor we passed to check for women. To try and set them free, even if I knew we weren't equipped.

We couldn't do anything without more forces and more power—at least not without incurring casualties, and that was an outcome I would never accept.

"I think I'm nearly strong enough to shift...what about you guys?" I asked my mates. Breaker shook his head, answering for both himself and my dad, who he was still supporting. Gage's look wasn't any more encouraging, pointedly glancing at my mom who was clutching him for support, one hand shielding her eyes, which were already squeezed shut. Olivia, who was riding piggyback on Fletcher and talking to Rachel, was doing something similar until Thomas draped his jacket over her head.

I couldn't imagine the strength it had taken for Carol to send her away, especially given that the girl had probably never left her mom's side before. And Olivia...had she even realized before now that there was a whole world outside the bars of her cell? An entire family she hadn't met?

"Once the wards disappeared, I began getting my magic back," Jagger said. "I could easily shift. Are you sure you can shift already, little treasure?" I heard my dad grumble in response to the nickname, which pulled the smallest smile onto my lips.

"I can try," I assured them, wanting to be as strong as my mates. "Mom, Dad, you'll probably have to ride on one of us, unless we want to try to get down to the main level."

"That's not a good idea," Rachel called out. "Come look."

Joining her and Rebecca at the edge of the building, a curse left my lips. Wolf shifters stood in the streets, looking up at the building with angry expressions. Linan stood out to me, his grim smirk filled with victory and amusement and a hint of malice. It was an uncomfortable contrast, to say the least.

"Bexley," he said, his voice amplified by some type of device. Or magic. My gaze darted around him, looking for the magic user that helped him, but I saw no one of note. "It's a shame you were only able to get yourself and your friends out."

My parents took places next to me so that we lined the edge of the building. Linan's face turned red, and the wolves stared in stunned silence. I didn't know if they knew who my parents were—maybe everyone had known, or maybe it was the energy they gave off that revealed their identity.

"Jericho. Ashley."

"Linan Clanguard. I was hoping you'd be dead by the time we got out," my mom said without blinking an eye. Even while wounded and weak

—*especially* while wounded and weak—the woman's confidence was inspiring. I'd always looked up to Celine Bronzeheart for her many amazing qualities, and I was starting to understand how she and my mom had been such good friends. They were very similar in some fundamental ways.

"You doubted our daughter," my dad added. "You thought she wouldn't have the strength to break herself *and* us out. You were wrong, Clanguard."

Linan chuckled, a note of tension in the sound. "I didn't *doubt* anything. I knew they'd be able to escape, and I knew they'd try to get you out—or at least find out about you."

"Why then?" I asked. Everyone's gaze turned to me. "Why after all this time? What was the point?"

"Because he couldn't access us," my mom surmised, her eyes narrowed. "Your dad's magic was protecting us, and because of that he couldn't reach us anymore. For whatever reason, he needs us. Probably something to do with this insane need for—"

"Power," Linan finished, smirking. "And now, Bexley, you've done what no one else could—even me. You have provided me with your mates, my own sons, six storm dragons, and a half-breed.

"Rebecca, it's unfortunate that you're still alive, but I plan to make you useful."

I took Rebecca's lead and ignored his jab. "You

won't be using anyone anymore—especially not the people I love."

"We're fucking done with this." Breaker's voice was hard as he suddenly ran towards the edge of the rooftop. I wondered if he would drop the three stories to the ground, but at the last second he shifted, somehow finding the strength to do so in the face of being cornered by Linan. His back claw hit the edge of the building, causing some of the facade to crumble. My dad chuckled, and I tore my gaze from my mate soaring through the air and followed his line of sight to Linan.

Who looked enraged. His face was contorted into an awful sneer, his eyes narrowed on Breaker's soaring form as a tremble went through him. It was as if he was about to shift, unable to control his rage at the concept that we might escape.

"Did you really think we'd be so weak that you could hold us forever?" Gage demanded, his dominant tone sending shivers down my spine. Before Linan could answer Gage, Breaker broke the visual space between us, pulling up alongside the building, Linan began shouting orders. Now we were working on borrowed time.

"Mr. And Mrs. Blackforge, you take Olivia and go with Breaker," Jagger said. "Fletcher, help them up. I'll shift and carry the others."

My parents wanted to argue, but everyone was already in motion, ensuring they were secure on my mate before Breaker broke away from the building and flew into the sky. Luckily, Linan hadn't seen Olivia yet, and I prayed we could ensure her safe departure before it became a problem. Jagger kissed me hard before shifting as well, people flooding into the building to try and stop our quick departure.

Electric currents jumped from the ground, aiming for Jagger, but he dodged them and was able to stop long enough for us to load Rachel, her mates, and Rebecca onto his back. When Jagger took off, the doors behind us burst open, leaving Gage and me to face our enemies.

"Don't fucking move!"

"Go. Now," Gage said, turning to face them and moving to block their view of me. The sky darkened to black, pellets of rain coming down like hail. Feeling an exhilarating thrill of adrenaline, I sprinted towards the edge of the rooftop and shifted. I didn't overthink it, didn't consider how tired I was—I just did it.

At the same time, Gage summoned a bolt of lightning which hit the building and nearly cut it in half. My power exploded in response as my dragon released a bellow that echoed through the air. I could almost taste the terror I caused, and I didn't for a moment feel guilty.

As I soared through the sky, a secondary roar vibrated the space around me, and I instantly knew that Gage had shifted as well. That he was airborne. The sounds of guns going off scared the hell out of me, so I looked down as I began to fly towards my other mates, pulling on our bonds as I sensed Gage catching up to me.

Victory swelled inside of me as every single one of us escaped the Clanguard pack lands. We had done it. We had absolutely done it...I just didn't know what would come next.

As Gage pulled up next to me, the storm grew worse, rain falling in torrents on the pack lands and city below us. Despite our escape—a victory, in my mind —I could feel my mates' disappointment through our bond. They didn't like to leave a fight and worried that Linan would consider it a win because we'd had to 'run.'

That couldn't be farther from the truth, though. Linan had underestimated us, and now it was going to be his ruin.

As we flew beyond the city limits and into the

clan lands, faces turned skyward. I used my enhanced vision to pay close attention to the main roads, noticing a large number of individuals carrying the Clanguard sigil moving from Silvershade territory toward the city.

It was as if Linan had been calling his people back to help handle us. I was slowly starting to get a better read on him, but his intentions and the way he chose to handle things didn't make sense to me half the time. I was so trapped in my thoughts that I found myself mildly surprised when we soared far past the clan lands, not even considering stopping there.

Instead, we continued to fly north to the rogue lands. As I pulled up next to Breaker, both of my parents were watching me in awe and giddy excitement. I felt a surge of pride at their attention, and I had to stop myself from showing off. Especially because I was aware my energy wouldn't last forever.

The adrenaline was fading, and I was growing tired, but there was no time to stop—the conflict for the day was far from done. If we were going to the rogue lands, we could possibly be facing a fight. We hadn't exactly had the most welcoming of receptions there originally, and then to come there fresh off a conflict, practically bringing it to their doorstep? I didn't think they'd appreciate that.

Yet I couldn't deny that it was probably one of the most secure and protected places to go. It felt right to regroup at the place that Linan had last destroyed. To come to terms with what we had to do next in the place where everything had been set into motion so many years ago.

Pushing ahead, I could feel my mates trying to speed up to keep up with me, but I wanted to reach the rogue lands first. I wanted to do my best to ease the tension, and since I had no one riding on me, it only made sense. I had no doubt Gage would be close behind me.

As I soared above the forested region towards the estate on the hillside, I saw and heard movement below—shifters returning, making haste towards the estate. Thunder clapped in the distance over the city, the clouds moving rapidly to follow the source of the power that had conjured them. By the time I landed, I was unsurprised to find everyone gathered in the courtyard. I had to hope my mates would land on the other side of the courtyard gates, where there was far more room for them to safely unload their riders.

My ears buzzed as the space around me grew loud with voices, questions thrown at me with abandon. People were worked up and confused, and I didn't even know how to start to explain. I ran a hand over my heart, feeling like I couldn't breathe. I desperately needed to recover. I may have gotten my power back, but the flight had pulled on my last reserves.

I was officially at empty, and this had *officially* been the longest day of my life.

"Silence!" Dyer, the leader of the rogue lands' population, quieted the group with a singular word. He stood next to Aurora on the stairs, looking at me in surprise.

"Bexley?" Aurora said as I wavered on my feet, taking a step towards me. But she stopped when an instant later Gage appeared behind me, holding my hip to steady me.

"Not just her—all of them," Dyer said as the other nine members of our group joined us. Instantly I could see that some individuals recognized my parents.

"What has happened to our home?" my dad asked, making me wince. It was possibly the worst thing he could have said. Some voices rose in panic as Dyer's gaze narrowed, but even more people looked on in shock at seeing the Flash clan leaders returned from the dead.

"It's not our home anymore," I said loudly, managing to quiet the crowd. "It's theirs. They live here now." My parents' expressions said that an explanation would be needed, but they held their objections. I turned back to Aurora and Dyer. "We need your help."

"Our help?" Aurora asked. "With what? Whatever chaos goes on in the city isn't our—"

"It is, though," Gage argued. "It *is* your problem. He'll come here next—war will reach your doorstep. We don't need you to fight if you don't want to, but we do need to use the rogue lands as a base to gather support and shelter anyone trying to escape the impending violence."

"We won't let this place fall again; we have families here. Entire lives built on these grounds." I was impressed that Dyer wasn't intimidated by my mates or my parents—the looks they were offering him couldn't be good.

"The battle won't happen here," Breaker assured him. "We'll meet Linan's forces in the dragon clan territories or go to the city. But we need a central command. My mate is asking politely," he added, placing special emphasis on the last word.

"I highly suggest you agree with her." Jagger said.

After a long moment of silence, Dyer nodded. "I can see that I don't have much choice here, and I don't appreciate the illusion. You may camp out on the main floor, but the families who live in the apartments won't be disturbed by strangers. The private suites from the Blackforge family before are still available to them. All we ask is that you won't wage war in the home it's taken us nearly a decade to build."

The last part seemed very pointed towards my parents.

"We promise," Breaker agreed.

"Linan will try to come here, so we have to act fast," my mom said. "He won't let this go, especially—"

"If he wants Bexley," Rachel volunteered, offering me a concerned look.

"Then let's call the others and have them meet us here. An official declaration of war needs to be made."

Suddenly, the voices around me turned hazy and muted, like I was hearing them from underwater. I felt unsteady on my feet, unable to find equilibrium. Stumbling, I lost my footing and would have fallen on my butt if Gage hadn't been right there to scoop me up and pull me against his chest.

"Cupcake? What's going on?"

"I think...I think I may have overdone it a bit with my magic." The world around me clicked off like a screen going dark.

Chapter 13

Bexley Blackforge

The hot water from the shower brought me back to life. And with that I *finally* felt fully aware after the extensive process I'd gone through to wake myself up.

I couldn't tell you how long I slept after I passed out, but when I woke up, it had taken me three times —falling asleep between each—to even fully open my eyes. When I managed to finally do so, I'd slowly rolled my body off the bed, my limbs feeling heavy like they were weighed down. I'd nearly given up at that point, despite knowing it was essential I get up. There were too many important things to be done...

On my way to the shower, I didn't disturb the heavy, drawn curtains in the unfamiliar bedroom, not wanting to wake Gage up. I imagined he and the others were just as tired as I'd been, although Jagger and Breaker were missing. I had no idea where they'd gone to; what I did know was that this shower had made me feel miraculously better and fully rejuvenated.

Tilting my head back, I let the water slide over my face as I reveled in stretching my sore body. Somehow, someway, I could sense that I was more powerful than before. Stronger. My magic was running under my skin in exhilarating forks of lightning, and while my mind was still moving a bit slow, I was awake enough to know that I needed to get moving.

There was entirely too much to deal with. Like an actual freakin' war, for one.

By now everyone had probably gathered here. Certainly the other storm dragon clan leaders would be here. Hopefully my parents had recovered enough to at least be able to greet their old friends and catch up with them—something I needed to do myself. I'd given my mom a short version of my story, and they'd probably heard several other people's versions by now, but I felt like I owed it to them to give my own full account. I knew my mom felt guilty about what I'd been through, and I wanted to dispel that. There was only one person to blame, and if my mates had anything to do with it, he wouldn't be long for the world.

"Cupcake?"

"Hey," I whispered as Gage stepped into the shower, my eyes running over his body and trying to not get turned on by his mere presence. *Of course, it didn't help that he was naked.* When he pulled me into his arms, I melted against him. A surge of desire overcame me at the feel of his hard length pressing between us. Apparently he wasn't very good at remaining unaffected either.

I whimpered as his hand came underneath my chin, tilting it up to examine my face. When his lips brushed against mine, I became absolutely entranced, his kiss hard and possessive. Trembling, my nipples hardening painfully as the hot water rolled over our bodies, I let my hand fall between us, sliding my fingers along his cock.

Feeling more bold than ever before, I began to stroke him slowly, his kisses becoming hungry as he tugged me to the bench of the shower, pulling me on his lap. No words were said as I climbed on top of him, poised to take what we both wanted. I whimpered as his lips traced down my chest, wrapping around my nipple and teasing the delicate peak with his teeth.

When he bit down on my breast, I nearly came on the spot, and a rumble released from his chest that vibrated through me.

"Come here," he demanded, tugging my hips downward. I hissed in relief as I began to slide down on him, my thighs trembling as his thick length stretched me.

"That's right, open up for me, cupcake," he rumbled, biting down on my lip. I whimpered, suddenly dropping my weight and sliding down the full length of his cock. *Holy fates.* I moaned against Gage's lips as I tightened around him, the slight sting of pain absolutely nothing compared to the rightness of feeling him deep inside of me.

It hadn't been that long since I'd lost my virginity to him, but it felt like forever. It felt like I had missed him being inside of me for years—decades. That was the type of need he inspired in me.

"You control the pace. I don't want to go too fast until you're ready," he said, running his hands through my hair and gathering it in a knot around his fist. With his encouragement I began to bounce up and down, his full length causing my body to clench in anticipation. The sensation was amazing, but I found myself frustrated, needing to feel him dominating me—pounding into me.

"Gage," I moaned against his lips, "I need faster —I need you to take over. Please."

That was all it took—a simple 'please.' I whimpered as I was suddenly pinned against the tile wall of the shower. I wrapped my legs around Gage's hips, holding on for dear life as he began to punch his hips forward, railing in and out of me. Faster. Harder. Everything I could have asked for. I screamed out his name as my nails dug into his skin, the scent of blood filling the air.

My climax slammed into me out of nowhere, sending me absolutely reeling.

And when his lips brushed over our mating mark? It felt like I was sent flying, soaring into the stratosphere. I was adrift in a cosmos of pleasure that was slowly drowning me in the sweetest way possible.

"Fuck—you feel so good squeezing around me, Bex," he snarled, slamming into me once—twice—before finally bottoming out and releasing deep inside of me. Gage's hand came down hard on the wall behind me, a loud *crack* making my eyes snap open. Then I was whisked away from the wall as Gage groaned, his cock flexing inside of me.

"Oh no." I burst into giggles, feeling almost a bit high, as I saw that a piece of tile had not only cracked but fallen off the shower wall. Gage chuckled and shook his head, burying his face against my neck. As the laughter subsided, Gage squeezed my ass before finally pulling out and setting me on my feet. Instantly I felt the loss.

"Sort of hot," I said when I noticed the red tinge of his ears, brushing my nose against his. I knew he wasn't really embarrassed about breaking the wall; it was more that he got caught up in the moment and forgot his own strength.

"All that matters is that you think that, cupcake... and that we find a good way to explain it."

"Explain what?" Jagger asked before dropping towels on the vanity. I could barely see him through the fog on the glass of the shower door, so I gave Gage a quick kiss and moved to open it. I jumped as he hit my butt and I half-heartedly scowled, feeling giddy. *Talk about stress relief.*

As I stepped out of the shower, Jagger wrapped a towel around me. The soft material felt good against my skin, and his icy eyes were filled with heat and amusement. I was glad that I didn't spot any signs of exhaustion lingering in his gaze.

"Gage cracked the tile in the shower," I said, going to brush my teeth. Jagger chuckled. "Did you just come back to the room?"

"Went to get you food. When you come out, you should eat something—you've been asleep for almost forty-eight hours."

My toothbrush—which was somehow the exact same as my old one—nearly fell out of my hand. "What?"

"Yeah." Gage shut off the water, and I handed him a towel before he stepped out. I chose to not stare at his amazing body covered in water droplets, but it was hard. And when Jagger kissed the shell of my ear, my attention began to really get tugged between the two of them. Deliberately averting my eyes, I applied toothpaste and stuck the toothbrush in my mouth. "A lot has changed, so you need to eat and get settled before we explain."

"Okay," I said around the toothbrush, both relieved and a little sad when they left. Trying to refocus on getting ready, I brushed out my hair and took the time to dry it, searching through the familiar bag of cosmetics. Celine or one of the other moms must have brought this—it contained every single product I normally used, down to the pack of makeup wipes. It was extremely thoughtful.

When I was done, I grabbed a cotton robe and put it on, walking out into a suite I didn't recognize. Jagger pointed out a pile of clothes, the sight of them confirming my suspicions—this was definitely Celine Bronzeheart's doing.

I sorted through the choices, picking a pair of blue cropped pants and a soft lavender sweater that clung to my curves. Slipping on a pair of no-show socks and flats, Jagger called me over to a couch where Gage was already sitting and eating. A large platter of food sat on the table, an assortment of everything from cheese to fruit to pastries available.

I happily sipped some coffee, sighing happily at the taste of peppermint on my tongue, before looking at my two mates. "Where's Breaker?"

"Talking with your dad."

"About what? The attack?"

"No. Breaker was the last to wake up, so he's most likely having the same conversation he had with the two of us separately—one I didn't think I would ever have the pleasure of participating in."

"Wait, what?" I frowned. Gage seemed amused as I tried to piece together what he meant.

"The 'you better treat my daughter right or I'll rip your head off' type of conversation," Jagger said as he handed me a plate with fruit and an orange scone.

I shook my head in disbelief. "There is no way." My eyes widened at their dry looks. "He didn't!"

"He said *worse*." Gage chuckled. "But that's okay. I'm just glad he's around to have that conversation with us—in fact, everyone is thrilled to have your parents back."

"My mom almost cried," Jagger agreed.

"My mom *did* cry." Gage shrugged. "Probably my dad too. He was best friends with yours—or maybe I should say *is* best friends."

I simply shook my head, wondering what that would be like, having parents who were friends. With my parents back, there was an entire layer of relationship dynamics that I didn't know or understand yet. I mean, even the concept of my dad having a 'fatherly' talk with my mates surprised me. I knew my mates were taking it in a relaxed and good-natured fashion, but it just seemed so odd to me. It felt foreign to be able to call them 'Mom' and 'Dad' in the first place—yet I did it with an ease, familiarity, and confidence that surprised me.

In a way, I was glad my memories had been removed for so long. If I'd lived eight years believing they were dead, it would have been even harder to wrap my head around than it was already proving to be.

"What else have I missed?" I asked curiously.

Jagger ran a hand over my back as he encouraged me to keep eating. "A declaration of war was sent out to everyone in the dragon clan territories, and our allies in the city have shared it with their people as well. A storm is overhead, and I think it's acting as a beacon because this place is packed with both people wanting to fight and people seeking shelter. The clan lands have been essentially cleared because we hope to wage war outside of the rogue lands—ideally within central clan territory where we have the advantage of having a good gauge on the landscape."

"How many people are we talking about?" I asked, considering the size of the estate. It could fit a lot of people, but at some point there simply wouldn't be enough beds in the actual building.

"Everyone from the clan lands, except for some that decided to stay in their homes to defend them if the war crosses their doorsteps. There's also the non-wolf shifters from the city, even though Linan will probably use their absence as an excuse to claim their sectors. Everyone is preparing for when Linan's troops begin moving out. We're now competing on a similar level to him when it comes to numbers, but our fighting styles will be more diverse and unpredictable compared to his."

"How long do you predict we have?" I asked softly, feeling a thread of nervousness. I was glad they appeared to have confidence in all of this, but the idea of a full-out war being waged wasn't one that would ever settle comfortably in my stomach.

"It's been two days since the notice was delivered to Clanguard, so not much longer." Which meant I needed to figure out my place in all of this— if I even had one.

"We should go find everyone else." I stood up and my mates seemed to agree, following me toward the door as I prepared myself for the chaos that would greet us.

* * *

At first we were only met with silence, the castle quiet as we worked our way down from the private quarters to the main floor. It was only then that I noticed it was nighttime. Stars twinkled in the sky—well, a few that managed to peek through the clouds did. They were so thick I could barely see the moon, and I wondered if everyone was already asleep in their rooms, lulled by the thunder rumbling in the distance.

When we arrived on the main floor, though, I realized I was right—everyone was sleeping—but not in separate rooms. There were hundreds of people camped out in the grand hall, sleeping on cots and in sleeping bags. Dimmed lanterns lit the walls, their flickering lights highlighting guards moving through their peaceful forms, keeping watchful, protective eyes on them.

Jagger motioned for us to follow him outside, and we were hit with a cool autumn wind that carried a familiar scent. My dragon nearly burst forth, frantic to get to my parents. My steps quickened as I searched for them, and thankfully it wasn't long before I spotted them across the front courtyard.

My mom turned from her conversation with Celine —I could only imagine that she'd felt my presence as I'd felt hers—and I couldn't help but break into a smile at seeing how much better she looked. How much more vibrant she looked. Her hair no longer hung limply, now surrounding her like a silver-streaked cloak. And while she was still far too thin, there was a healthy glow to her.

I was careful when I hugged her in greeting, not wanting to squeeze her too hard, but she didn't have the same concern, her arms holding me in a vise grip.

"You're finally up," she whispered, her voice thick with emotion as she pulled back from the hug. "Your dad and I were so worried."

"I heard he was so worried he decided to have a conversation with my mates?" I teased.

There was a mischievous glint to her gaze that I remembered from my childhood. "That may be true —although he and Breaker are over there laughing, so if he was trying to be scary, it didn't work."

A sudden sniff reminded me that Celine was nearby, watching both of us with a tearful smile.

"Oh, don't cry," I said in concern, grabbing her hand as my mom motioned for us to sit at the table they'd been occupying.

"I'm just so happy to be a part of this, to see you two reunited."

"Which is only possible because you did such an amazing job raising my daughter," my mom said, voice ringing with conviction. "I can't thank you enough for that, Celine. I can never repay you."

"No such thing—Bexley was amazing to raise. I got to put all my girly tendencies on her." She said the last part teasingly, but it was one hundred percent accurate. When Gage and his father had been off doing whatever male storm dragons did to bond, she and I had been off on our own doing an assortment of 'girly' things like shopping or gardening. But we also did other things together, like going hiking. Celine had been absolutely fundamental in making me the woman I was today.

"Bexley, girly? Never." My mom laughed, and I watched as the two of them talked as if no time had passed—as if they'd spent these past eight years side by side.

My other mates had joined my dad and Breaker, their parents—aside from Celine—floating between conversation with them and discussion of battle strategy with a group of soldiers poring over maps. The atmosphere was relaxed, but the plans were still being altered and changed, probably based on whatever intel they were gathering about Linan's preparations.

Now that I looked closer, I didn't see anyone else out here that I recognized. "Hey, where's Rachel? And her mates? Or Olivia?"

"Sleeping in a private suite, resting as much as possible," Celine explained. "It was just reported that Linan is moving his troops into formation."

"I'm glad I woke up," I murmured. "How's Olivia doing?"

"Adjusting. She's got her days and nights mixed up, and she misses her mom. Cries for her often. But your friend Rachel has done an amazing job keeping her occupied," my mom said. She paused, taking a breath before changing the topic. "Bexley...I need to ask you something. Or ask something of you, I should say."

"Yeah?" I asked curiously.

"I don't want you to fight." When I didn't give an immediate reaction, she added, "I know that's a lot to ask, especially with everything Linan has done. But if he's after you, the last thing we want to do is put you right in his line of sight."

"I know," I said, understanding. "That's fine. I'm not a fighter, but I will protect those that are here. I don't want anyone stepping foot into this place."

"Your daughter is a pacifist," Celine explained.

"She doesn't believe in shifter hierarchy either. Thinks it's bullshit."

"It is," my mom agreed, pride shining in her gaze. "I am so proud of you Bexley."

"You are? Why?" I couldn't deny it felt so good to hear those words leave her lips.

"Because of the woman you've become—one I can't wait to get to know."

No matter what came tomorrow, I would make sure we had that chance.

Chapter 14

Bexley Blackforge

A part of me had always recognized that I was not only sheltered but rather naive when it came to how the world worked. I'd been fortunate enough to live in a protective bubble after escaping from Linan that first time, but it had only been an extension of how I'd been raised initially. I didn't fault my parents or the Bronzehearts for that, or even society for encouraging it—it was only natural to want to protect your children. And because we were storm dragons, we as 'children' were considered even more important to society. It didn't surprise me that our safety and happiness had been held in such high regard—that I had been placed on a pedestal.

However, while I was thankful for those who'd protected me...right now I seriously wished I'd had a bit more 'tough' love. Or been placed in more stressful situations. Or even had more training. Because at this moment, more than anything, *I was envious.*

I was jealous of the skillset Breaker exhibited and the way he moved about, confidently handling weaponry before passing it off to others, ensuring that everyone had a piece of artillery they felt comfortable wielding.

Jealous at the ease with which Jagger handled our parents as they discussed military strategy and how to protect those who'd come seeking shelter from the impending battle.

Jealous at the way Gage commanded people, his orders never called into question, inspiring unwavering support from anyone he spoke to.

I was just so incredibly envious of their experience and training.

Instead of helping in a productive way, I felt forced to stand to the side, watching as everyone moved around me, the estate coming alive in anticipation. The dawn light had traveled across the courtyard in the hours since I'd woken up, seeping through the windows of the great hall and waking everyone.

It was clear who planned to fight and who didn't, because those ready for battle immediately reported to the courtyard. My gaze tracked over the hundreds of individuals gathered, having lost my mates in the crowd as they helped organize the troops. Aquatic shifters. Avian shifters. Feline shifters. Rogue wolf shifters. Even some prey shifters who were wielding weapons themselves, going against their base instincts to aid in defeating Clanguard. It was a bit overwhelming, the scale of it all, and even standing at a distance on the stairs I didn't feel like I had enough air to breathe.

Or maybe it was because I felt utterly useless with no way to help and nothing to do.

I'd been able to spend some time aiding inside, ensuring that families seeking refuge here received breakfast and that they had everything they needed before we locked down the building. After that, I'd gone back to feeling useless.

I'd tried to help the moms, who were currently bent over a map of the pack lands, coordinating the plan on how to release the women trapped in Clanguard's prison. But my voice seemed to disappear when I tried to offer advice, leaving the military generals staring at me in confusion. Clearly thinking that I didn't belong.

And maybe they were right. Maybe I didn't belong here—and I sure didn't belong on the battlefield. So why did a part of me so desperately want to go?

"Overwhelmed?" Aurora asked as she joined me on the front steps of the estate, her hands in her pockets as she examined the gathered forces. I had no idea what would come next for the rogue lands after the war—assuming we won—but despite their initial objections, she and Dyer had been helping in any way they could.

"Sort of. I don't really know what I'm supposed to be doing," I answered honestly, figuring she wouldn't have asked if she didn't really want to know. "This entire time I've had a purpose, whether it was finding Rebecca or helping release my parents, but now...well, now war is at our doorstep, and I have absolutely no idea how to help.

"I know what my mates would say—they'd claim that my part's done and that I just need to stay safe, but that doesn't sit right with me."

Aurora considered my statement for a long moment. "Right. Well, here's something for you to do: we have a castle full of people that want nothing to do with this war but need protecting from it. Help with that. While we appreciate the effort you've put into keeping the fighting away from here, I think we all know there's a high chance that Linan will find a way to break through the front line and end up here. *That's* when you'll need to fight."

Her words resonated with me—it was, after all,

what I told my mom I'd do just last night. So why didn't it feel like enough? I still felt guilty for not being on the front line, but Aurora was right. This is where I needed to be, and I'd need to be strong if Linan somehow found his way here. If he was looking for me, which he seemed to be, it was very possible it would come to that—an outcome my mates were completely refusing to consider, determined to ensure it never occurred.

A familiar laugh filled the air, and I turned to see Rachel coming downstairs with Olivia at her side. I'd seen Fletcher and Thomas alongside my mates, but this was the first time I'd seen my friend since I passed out. As she walked towards us, her face lit up with relief.

"Bexley!" Rachel pulled me into a hug. "I'm so glad to see you're up. Are you feeling better?"

"Much better," I admitted before crouching down to look at Olivia. Her milky gaze stared right at me from beneath the hood of her pink cloak, shielding her from light. "And how are you feeling?"

"Okay," she murmured. "I miss my mommy though."

"I promise we'll bring her safely to you," I assured her.

I didn't get a chance to say anything else, though, before a roar bellowed through the air, causing everyone's eyes to go skyward. *Oh.* My eyes widened at the whoosh of wind passing over wings, dark figures dotting the sky. There had to be at least fifty of them.

Somehow I'd forgotten that other dragons existed. I hadn't been exposed to them much while growing up with the Bronzehearts, but they lived within clan lands. Apparently, according to my parents, a large percentage of our population had been killed off during the attack on the Flash clan. Despite being able to live in any of the dragon clan lands, many dragon shifters had preferred the Flash lands because of the higher elevation. It also explained why I hadn't seen many dragons around—even within the Bronzeheart estate.

These were the ones left.

I watched in awe as they soared above the estate. Their magic was exhilarating, rushing against my skin, and I had to resist the sudden urge to shift. To join them.

It was impossible to ignore.

"They're patrolling the skies, keeping an eye out for when Linan begins to march north," Rachel explained. "They were further south, but if they're back it means our forces need to leave soon."

I jogged inside and up the stairs, knowing exactly where I wanted to go. On the third floor, I went to a balcony that overlooked the courtyard and watched the figures in the sky swoop gracefully through the air, the cloudy skies causing them to stand out in dazzling effect.

They were magnificent.

"Bexley!" one of my mates growled, their voice loud above the crowds gathered, but I was already over the railing and jumping off the balcony, shifting mid-air. Thunder cracked and lightning struck as my skin hardened to scales and the dragon within me was released.

Welcoming roars greeted me as I flew towards the other dragons, a wave of excitement and cheers sounding from below. A light drizzle coated my scales, and dragons moved out of my way as I shot up and circled around, letting my eyes greedily soak up the details of the other dragons up close and personal.

Magenta. Purple. Navy. Crimson. White. There were so many of them and in so many colors, each of them varying in wingspan, size, and power. Some had horns, and others didn't. Some had large wings meant for gliding, and others had smaller wings for speed. It was fascinating!

As I flew around a group of three smaller dragons, each of them offering me rumbles in greeting, I felt a sense of pure joy. These were my kin, my own species. Of course the Bronzehearts had always made me feel part of something, but this...there was something more base to this. Connecting to these other dragons, these other creatures who were just like me, was special. It also gave me hope that between them and the forces on the ground, the war would be over quickly. There was no way Linan could match us.

My attention turned south at the thought of him, and that was when I saw it—the reason the dragons had flown back in the first place.

Lights speckled the land, moving in a large group. Now that I was paying attention, I could feel the power shifting through the air as Linan's massive army moved into position, coming for us on the offense. I had no idea how his pack had grown so large—maybe it had always been this size—but it was a formidable force.

My thoughts moved back to when Trek had mentioned being able to end all of this instantly. Was that an option anymore? Far more lives would be lost through this battle than any power surge storm dragons could cause, but if we could target Linan...

No. If that was a possibility, they would've already enacted it.

Death was unavoidable. It was a raw and painful reality that brought me down to earth—literally—shifting as I dropped down outside of the courtyard.

Breaker was waiting for me as I walked through the gate, concern written plain on his face. When he brought me into his arms, I tilted my head back to look into his eyes.

"We're leaving soon. We want to meet him before he reaches the edge of the territory."

"Why do you need to go?" I whispered, suddenly worried for my mates. With the exception of my own, all of the other dads were going, as well as Breaker's mom, but that didn't make me feel better. That just meant that more people I cared about were in potential danger. More people that I could lose when I'd just gotten *everything* back.

"Hey," Breaker said, smoothing his fingers over my cheek. "I promise we will do our best to focus our attacks on those who want this war, not the others who've been caught up in it—not the ones being forced to fight."

"I know it's unavoidable," I admitted. "I would rather you three come home safe, even if it means killing others. I feel horrible saying that."

"Don't feel horrible about that," Breaker said forcefully. "I would burn this world for you, Bex. In a heartbeat."

I was glad to hear it, but I hoped it wouldn't come to that.

* * *

Half an hour later I was standing between my mates as they laid out the plan. My back was pressed against Gage's chest as his hand smoothed over my hip in a repetitive and comforting pattern. Jagger watched my expression closely, picking up on my tension as Breaker spoke. I could tell they were trying to make me feel better by including me in the discussion as much as possible, but I wasn't sure if it was making me feel better or worse. If it was alleviating my concern or just putting visuals of the imagined scenarios in my head.

"We're going to stop them before they reach the rogue land border. We want the majority of their forces to stay in dragon clan territories," Breaker explained. "Dragons and avians will attack aerially, and the rest will stay on the ground. We have weaponry, but half of the forces will fight in shifted form so that we can rely on both forms of attack."

"We're hoping nothing hits here; however, we will have a medical team set up at the entrance of the estate, so there will be no need for us to unlock the gates once the fighting starts," Jagger added.

"Breaker!" His dad called. Breaker gave him a sharp nod, and I knew it was time for them to go. I surged forward and wrapped my arms around him, hugging him tight as he smoothed a hand through my hair. As I tilted my head back, he pressed a kiss to my lips and whispered that he loved me before I finally released him. Jagger smoothed a hand up my back as I watched Breaker walk away.

"It will be completely fine," Jagger promised. "Don't you worry, little treasure."

"I'm going to worry," I told him, looking into his familiar gaze. "You're my mates, the loves of my life. I can't *not* worry."

Jagger cast me a small smirk and dipped his head, brushing his lips over mine. "Well I can't argue when you say that."

"Just be safe. I love you."

"I love you too," he said, following Breaker to the front line of the forces preparing to leave.

Gage turned me in his arms, and I stared up into his handsome face, my hands tightening on him, wondering if there was a way to convince them to stay. "Do not take any risks, cupcake. No matter what you feel through our bond, we will absolutely be okay."

"You can't ask that of me." I shook my head, feeling distressed already. I shouldn't take any risks?! What about them?

"None of us will be able to focus if we think you're in danger. Promise me."

"I promise," I whispered, unable to help myself. "Please be careful, Gage. Please? He killed dragons before; he can do it again."

Gage's kiss was hard and demanded all of my attention. It made my mind go completely blank as I melted into him with a happy sigh. When he finally pulled away, his voice was so incredibly serious. "I love you, Bex. We're ending this today."

"I love you, Gage."

As he walked away, I waved to the others who were going, my arms wrapping around myself as I tried to maintain a brave face. I didn't want them to doubt for a minute that I believed in them.

When the war horns sounded from afar, everyone began to move at once. I felt lost in a wave of people being jostled, and as I stood there, frozen— desperately wanting to call my mates back—the courtyard cleared out.

"Come inside, honey," Celine said. They were waiting on me to close the doors. With one last, long look at the departing forces, I stepped inside. The doors slammed shut, and without a word I trailed up the stairs. Someone called my name, but I kept moving. I knew exactly where I wanted to be for all of this.

When I reached the topmost floor, I stepped onto the balcony and surveyed the land. I could mark where our troops were based on the dragons in the sky, as well as the flags from all the different clans and packs who marched to war. When they broke through trees, I could see our forces moving like a wave across the land. Closing my eyes, I sent a prayer up to the fates that everything would be okay. That my mates would return to me.

Linan Clanguard's attack was going to end far differently than it had last time.

Chapter 15

Breaker Firespell

Size can be your greatest disadvantage on the battlefield.

I had found that statement was true in both my dragon and my human forms. Those words, shouted at me by my father on an ungodly hot summer afternoon when I was sixteen, had stuck with me for so long—mostly *confusing me*. At the time, I hadn't truly understood what he meant. Then, when I found myself in real-life battle situations, it became clear.

In most situations in life, I dominated the space with my size alone, putting aside anything having to do with my magic—but with it? And with my dragon? Even more so. The same concept didn't apply as well on the battlefield, though, because the biggest individual wasn't always the biggest threat, especially in hand-to-hand combat.

Other shifter species, especially wolves, had mastered the art of changing back and forth between their creature and human forms. They could make the transition in seconds flat, in the narrowest of spaces. It made them hard to target and particularly lethal. They weren't a sitting target like a dragon would be on the ground, too big to move fast and lacking a natural agility when not in the air. But there were only a limited type of attacks we could effect from the sky—unless we planned to kill everyone, our side included.

So I hadn't shifted. Instead, I stayed in my human form and pulled on every ounce of training I had, the heavy sword in my hand slicing through the air effortlessly. As my sword came down on some unlucky individual, a clean slice through the back of their neck causing them to drop to their knees as their head rolled elsewhere, I found myself thankful for the training my father had drilled into me day in and day out.

It hadn't been fun by any stretch of the imagination, but it had been necessary. Necessary to ending this.

The morning light was replaced by darkness as storm clouds thickened overhead, a dark chuckle leaving my father as he stabbed someone before turning sharply and impaling another with a dagger. My mother scowled at him, removing her sword from the individual's chest and kicking the body away.

"I had that covered!" she shouted.

"Just supporting you," he claimed, looking damn near giddy as they worked their way through the masses. Around us the chaos of war raged, and while I couldn't see Gage or Jagger, I knew they were close. Considering the amount of anger surging through them, I had a feeling they'd caught sight of Linan. Hopefully they wouldn't mind when I found him and ended him first...

Mowing through another three individuals, the *clang* of metal on metal ringing in my ears, my eyes narrowed on a group of figures in the distance, looking over each individual. I knew it would be hard to spot him, but—

There he fucking was. In the middle of it all.

Something that surprised me considering what a coward he was, whether he would admit to that or not. I could see the cockiness in his gaze as the men around him fought. He held a sword in his hand but didn't lift it once, the protective barrier of bodies around him doing all the work. And they were doing excellent work—it was clear his wolves had training, using a specially formed technique of combat combined with shifting back and forth so efficiently that landing a hit on them was nearly impossible. It was also hard to predict how they would attack you, to know if you needed to watch for a sword or a bite.

Even from the sky, where the avian shifters and dragons were attempting diving attacks and raining down elemental surges of power, the wolves were doing a damn good job at avoiding any lethal blows. I was glad for the amount of reinforcements we had ended up with, because without them I wouldn't be nearly as confident about the outcome of this conflict.

I wasn't as interested in the larger battle at hand, though, and as I worked my way toward Linan, I allowed my rage to grow. The things this bastard wanted to do to my mate—*the love of my life*. The thought was all it took to turn my temper white-hot as I brutally killed each wolf in my way. Knowing that Bexley was safe, that she was far away from here, did little to make me feel better. I knew his goal. I knew that Linan was not only after this realm and its power, but her. This was the end of the line for all of it—*for every single dream of his.*

"Clanguard!" My voice was loud and harsh as he snapped his gaze toward me. I felt satisfied at seeing fear grow in his gaze, and before he could call more reinforcements, a wave of our people surged forward and met his current wall. It allowed me to get closer, looming near as if the shadow of death itself was coming for the bastard.

He deserved worse than death.

"Firespell," he spit. I offered him a sadistic grin before charging at him with my sword. For a singular moment, I wondered if he would run—or possibly shift—but when the collision of metal reverberated through the air and my sword hit his, excitement and adrenaline at the prospect of true battle slammed into me.

"Funny. I thought you would run like a bitch," I bit out as I pulled back, swinging once more as our dance of swords began. Clanguard didn't have my skill, but he was faster, able to dodge my blows, even if only by hair's breadth. If he didn't dodge them, he met them with his sword. I pushed forward, the *clang* of our swords causing him to stumble back. He bent under the weight as he turned sharply and dislodged his weapon from mine, darting out of the way.

"You're the one who's losing here, Breaker. You've already lost." *Clang*. Again and again the sound echoed like a battle drum, urging me forward as we exchanged blows.

Clang.

"I see more of your blood being shed than ours," I

argued. *Clang.* "Also, we have what you want: the territory and Bexley."

"Keep your territory," he spit. *Clang.* "All I need is the whore. We can worry about power later."

His words had their intended effect, *but* he didn't expect my physical reaction—surging forward with a hit hard enough to knock him onto the ground, the tip of my sword slicing across his chest. He growled, blood streaming from the cut like a river, as I shifted out of the way, an arrow shooting past me from someone trying to pull my attention. Unfortunately, the millisecond of distraction was just long enough for Linan to recover.

"You do not speak about her. Ever." My voice had the individuals around us scattering mid-fight, and I could see the creature inside Linan respond in fear. To his credit, he gripped his sword tighter as I repositioned myself, trying to establish a predictable pattern that would allow me to land a fatal blow.

"I'll speak of her all I want. She'll create an entire litter of storm dragons for me—"

I snapped.

With an enraged roar, I charged. He dodged, but only barely, my sword ripping across his arm. He cursed as his movements grew sluggish, his endurance absolutely nothing compared to mine.

Still, he had life to him. He could still escape. He could still go and find Bexley.

"You will never have Bexley," I snarled. *Clang.* "And your heirs have abandoned you. You have nothing, Clanguard."

"You think those pathetic children are my only option?!" He chuckled, his cheeks turning red. *Clang.*

"Right," I bit out. *Clang.* "We have Olivia as well, though."

Linan stumbled back, wide-eyed and tripping over his own feet. I smiled as his face turned purple, his eyes darkening. "What did you just say?"

"He said that we have your brat." My father appeared next to me as Linan let out a furious roar and charged forward. Before I could raise my sword, my father met him head on, warning that I should look behind me.

Fuck.

A massive bastard, almost seven feet tall, shifted into his wolf form on the spot and darted towards me. I didn't hesitate to bring down my sword hard as I slid to the side, dragging it across his ribs—hoping to see his guts spill across the battlefield.

Unfortunately, it didn't leave a fucking mark, his skin like metal. *It did absolutely fucking nothing.* As the bastard passed me, he shifted back into human form, his dagger grazing me. I hissed in pain, but it refocused me, adrenaline sharpening everything into absolute clarity.

Clang.

Clang.

Clang.

Our battle raged for what felt like hours, neither of us giving an inch. I had to admit that out of all of those I'd fought, he was likely the best. His endurance seemed endless. When I heard a sudden roar of frustration, I snapped my head over to find my father holding his abdomen, a group of individuals surrounding him.

Linan was nowhere to be found, though. Completely gone. It was a fucking ambush—the coward.

Darting away from the enemy attacking me, I only got a few feet away when a dagger flew past me and hit one of his own damn men. With a growl, I turned around and lodged my sword deep in his chest, his closeness from trying to catch me off guard working to my advantage. Twisting the metal and creating a hole in his chest, I felt immense satisfaction as I ripped it out and kicked him to the ground. *Bastard.*

When I reached my father, he'd fallen to a knee, pressing his hands firmly to his gut. Gage and Jagger were helping clear the area around him, keeping Linan's forces from taking advantage.

"Medical. Now," I shouted to one of our men, giving a warning look to my father as he attempted to stand.

"Absolutely not." He ripped away his shirt, my grimace unavoidable at the blood pouring from him.

"You are a stubborn old man."

"I'm serious," he argued, holding my gaze. "There are people who need it more than me. I'm already healing." Looking past the blood, I saw that he was right—the skin was grafting together as it did usually for dragons. But still, he needed to go back to the estate, not be on the damn battlefield at his age, injured.

When he grabbed my shirt and spoke to me in a hard tone, I was brought back to my childhood, listening to every damn command he gave. "Linan escaped. He's going to the estate. Now that he knows his daughter's there—"

"Fuck." I hadn't considered that. I should have—

"Go," my dad implored. "Go now. Find him before he gets there."

"Come with me."

With an uncharacteristic smile, he brought his sword up once more. "And miss out on all of this? No. Now go kill that bastard." He charged forward into the crowd, and I recognized in that moment there was absolutely no stopping him.

Fuck it.

Looking up to the sky and making sure there was no one close enough to harm, I shifted Soaring up and past the other dragons, I released a roar that I hoped would strike fear into Linan. It didn't take long for me to catch his scent, but the minute I did I realized he was running right toward the estate in shifted form.

Right toward Bexley.

Chapter 16

Bexley Blackforge

"What are you doing?" Gage asked as I placed another stitch into the fabric. I looked at the horizon through the open balcony doors, then back down at my needlework. The thread was the right shade of orange, but I still didn't like it.

"I'm trying to create a sunset, but I don't love the color."

My friend sat down next to me, examining the piece before assessing my collection of thread. Picking up two spools, he held them next to one another in the light.

"Could you intertwine them somehow and do both colors so that it blends?"

"Oh." I tilted my head in thought. "It would be double the stitch size, probably, but I'll try. That's a great idea."

"*You may have to do it after dinner. Our parents are ready, and the others just arrived.*"

"*Wait! Jagger and Breaker are here? Why didn't you freakin' lead with that?*"

Gage scowled, having been particularly grumpy this trip compared to normal. Not with me, exactly, but with pretty much anyone else around us...which was weird since Jagger and Breaker were his best friends.

Come to think of it, they'd almost gotten into a physical fight last time we were all together, but no one would tell me what it had been about.

"*They're always around. Nothing special.*" He shrugged, looking suddenly frustrated.

Offering him a confused look, I placed down my stitching and stood, walking onto the balcony and peeking my head over to see both of their carriages in the driveway. Turning, I found Gage right behind me, offering me another look I didn't fully understand.

"*Spending time with any of you is special to me,*" I countered.

His gaze warmed, and he let out a long sigh, conceding. "*I know, I know. Come on, let's go see them.*"

. . .

That was exactly what I wanted to do right now—*to go see them.*

I stood on the exact same balcony, my hands gripping the cement railing. That memory—a clear display, I now realized, of them all having feelings for me and not knowing how to deal with it—felt like a different life. It *was* a different life: one that wasn't filled with war and potential heartbreak.

Rolling forward on the tips of my toes, I felt the urge to shift. To go find my mates.

The things I felt through our bond didn't make me feel better about the situation, either.

Pain, for one. Not extreme pain, but enough to have me spinning anxious circles in my head, wondering how bad it had to be for me to feel *any* of it. Biting down on my lip a bit too hard, I tasted blood. I had to keep reminding myself that going to them would only make it worse. Then they'd be worried about my safety, distracted by their concern, and I wouldn't jeopardize everyone's well-laid plan just because I wanted to be near my mates.

Plus, the people inside were relying on me for protection. Well, not just me—Rachel, Celine Bronzeheart, Marilyn Silvershade, my dad, and my mom were here as well. I could hear voices from downstairs, and I wasn't surprised when my dad's magic reached out to me, his footsteps slow and steady as he walked into the room.

Despite having been imprisoned for eight years, each of my parents had managed to retain large parts of their personality, including humor. Not only that, but they were starting to look much more like themselves. Simple things like taking a shower, having a good meal, and getting some truly restful sleep—sleep not plagued by the looming threat Linan had posed—had made a world of difference.

"Bex?"

"Hey." I turned and offered him a small smile, trying not to portray my nerves.

He wasn't buying it. His face, the features so similar to the ones I saw in the mirror every day, said it all.

As he slowly sat down on a chair, I joined him across the coffee table. Unfortunately, sitting down did absolutely nothing to help me relax. If anything, it made me a bit more uneasy, my feet bouncing to expel the extra energy.

"You're worried about them," he observed. "And you're as bad about hiding that shit as I am. Your mother was always the one who could conceal her emotions."

"Really?" Being easy to read wasn't something I

wanted at the moment, but I was still happy to have something in common with my dad.

"Really." He chuckled. "After we started dating, it took a long time until I was convinced that she loved me as much as I loved her."

"No way. Mom seems pretty emotional and open, at least with me."

"Now," he agreed, his expression moving from amused to something more serious. "But growing up, she was very different—she didn't have the easiest life. Your grandparents were difficult."

"How so?" I asked. I was fascinated, wanting to know everything there was to know about my parents—and it certainly didn't hurt that I was currently in need of distraction. It was hard to imagine my mom as someone who wasn't emotionally vulnerable considering my memories of her and what I'd experienced recently, but it made sense in a way.

I surely would be different in twenty or thirty years than I was now.

"They were very traditional, wanted her out of the house and married from the time she turned eighteen." He grunted, settling himself further in the chair. "Luckily, I was able to make that happen since I met her about two days before."

"What?" I squeaked. "You got married in two days?!"

I mean, don't get me wrong, I loved that he knew my mom was the one—but even to me that seemed a bit extreme.

He chuckled. "Something like that. She moved in with me, at least. Took her a while to actually come around to liking me. I think I was over-whelming or something."

"It sounds like you may have kidnapped her," I teased.

He flashed a smile. "That sounds about right... but by the time our wedding rolled around, I had *totally* convinced her we were meant to be."

I broke out into a laugh, unable to stop myself. The twinkle in his eye told me he was only partially joking, making me wonder if he wasn't just a little bit crazy. I loved their love story, though, especially knowing that their connection to each other hadn't faded. From my dad protecting my mom with his magic all these years, to her being so fiercely protec-tive over him in return...I looked up to them in every way.

Looking out the window, my eyes trailing over the horizon, I let out a small sigh after our laughter died down. "I didn't realize how hard it would be to love someone. The loving part is easy, but the constant worry...it's a lot." And I knew my mates worried even more than me!

"And it only gets worse the longer you're together," he admitted. "But you're doing amazing. I mean, the fact that you haven't left yet says everything to me. I would've followed them minutes after they left."

He probably didn't realize just how close I'd been to doing exactly that.

I offered him a pointed look. "*Which reminds me*—my mates said you had a talk with them?"

An amused glint filled his eyes as he shrugged. "Nothing they couldn't handle. The conversation I had with them when you were younger and always playing together was probably worse. Until I trusted them, I was constantly worried that you were going to get caught up in one of their fights or something like that."

"They would never," I huffed. "Well, I'm not sure about then, but now at least."

"I swear, being a girl dad is not for the faint of heart." He shook his head looking momentarily distressed.

"What are you complaining about in here?" my mom teased, walking in and sitting on the arm of his chair. "Being a girl dad was *anything* but hard! You were always getting to relax and go on exciting adventures with us."

"That's true," he conceded, "but there was the constant worry—can't get rid of that. Something the other fathers will never understand. Not fully."

I'm sure they worried about their sons as well, but I understood his point—in the shifter world, there was quite a big difference between the dominance that someone like Breaker brought to the table compared to myself.

"But their sons might one day," I chirped, clapping a hand over my mouth the moment the words had left my lips. Had I literally just said that? *Time to backtrack.* "I mean, if we ever have kids or anything."

My mom burst out laughing as my dad grumbled under his breath and shook his head. "You know what," he huffed, "that may make me feel a little bit better. Then they'll understand where I'm coming from."

Before I could tease him further, a small scream that was instantly muffled had me sprinting onto the balcony. My eyes darted across the courtyard. I didn't see anything out of the ordinary, but I hadn't imagined that sound. I jumped and shifted mid-air without a moment of hesitation, searching the ground and locking onto a faint movement in the trees right within the western estate border. Shifting back, I dropped to the ground in a crouch and jogged over.

Opening my senses, I heard a rustling sound and creeped along the stone wall of the estate, trying to sneak up on anyone trying to break in. My body froze as my hand grazed over a particular stone marked with carved initials.

"We shouldn't be doing this," a feminine voice said. "We can't...you're part of Clanguard's pack. I live all the way out here; it doesn't even make sense."

"Shh. It's okay, baby. I promise that this will work out—we love each other, don't we?"

I looked around, finally finding the two people who were talking, their fingers intertwined and her back against the same stone wall. Aurora and a man I didn't recognize. His dark clothing was nondescript, but the scar down his face was violent.

"We do. Of course we do," she said. "You really think there's going to be war? The girl—Bexley. She said she didn't want that."

"That girl has no idea what she's involved in," he growled, and it took a moment for him to compose himself again. "Promise me something. When the

attack happens, meet me at the gates. I'm going to get us out of here. We'll go to another territory—"

The memory was ripped away as another scream sounded, my eyes snapping open. I traced the carved initials with a finger, one of them an 'A.' What had Aurora gotten herself into?

Continuing my search along the wall, I tried to make sense of what I'd just seen and how. It wasn't until I turned the corner and laid eyes on the two people in question that I was able to piece together what happened.

Aurora was unconscious and being held by a man wearing a Clanguard pack uniform, his expression filled with disgust. "Dumb bitch will believe anything." He dropped her on the ground and shoved his boot against her side, causing her to whimper.

The shifting of my feet on the dead leaves beneath me had the jerk looking up, right at me. "Well look who we have here. You must be the dragon, right?"

"Did you kill her?" My voice was foreign, etched in a fury that I didn't think was possible, considering Aurora and I were practically strangers. But everything about this...it felt so wrong. He'd betrayed her in the most fundamental way.

"No, but I will."

My dragon broke free from my control, and I didn't even bother to rein her back in. I ran forward and slammed my palm against his chest, his blood-curdling scream thrilling my dragon as the scent of burning skin filled the air. His eyes widened to the point they almost appeared to pop out before he fell to the ground....nearly, if not completely, dead.

I wanted to hesitate in the wake of what I'd just done, but my dragon didn't let me dwell on it. I had more urgent matters to tend to at the moment anyway. I kneeled next to Aurora, placing two fingers on the side of her neck. Her pulse thrummed, and I let out the breath I'd been holding. *She was alive.* Unconscious, but alive.

Aurora was taller than me but fairly light, so I picked her up the best I could and began to carry her back to the estate. The adrenaline rush from the altercation was fading, and I wondered how Aurora would feel when she woke; if she would remember what had happened. I wasn't even sure she would believe me, but hopefully...hopefully she would at least listen. She wasn't exactly my biggest fan to begin with, and now that I'd killed—

I couldn't even finish that sentence in my mind.

Guilt tried to seep in, but I forced it down. There were plenty of things people did in war that they wouldn't ever consider otherwise. He was hurting Aurora, and he'd been about to hurt me. I had no choice...so why did my eyes sting as if I was going to cry?

I was panting with effort by the time I reached the courtyard, struggling with the awkward effort of carrying another person. Pausing to shift Aurora into a position that would hopefully be more comfortable, I was struck by the eerie silence. Of course the doors to the estate were closed, so that made sense, but the medical team that had been stationed outside the gate was...gone? And the gate was busted open. Had I missed that when looking down on the courtyard initially?

Placing Aurora down, I walked to the gate and inhaled sharply, seeing specks of blood on the stone. The hair on the back of my neck rose as I tried to maintain composure, not wanting to show my nerves in case someone was watching. Returning to Aurora, I eyed the balcony—which was also empty. Had my parents gone back inside?

Maybe I could shift and bring Aurora up with me. The last thing I wanted was anyone opening the estate doors and potentially putting everyone in danger. Aurora's friend may have brought others with him. They could be circling the grounds now, waiting for a chance...

The front doors of the estate creaked open.

"Bexley Blackforge."

Standing at the top of the stairs, soldiers lining the space behind him and keeping everyone inside prisoner, was Linan Clanguard.

Chapter 17

Bexley Blackforge

"How?" It was the only question that came to mind as I tried to hide the tension and fear in my voice, my gaze holding his. I couldn't see past the soldiers surrounding him, their attention mostly on the crowd behind them. I could, however, feel those he held captured, their terror marking the air around us.

I felt physically sick. I'd failed at my job. Somehow we'd missed something. Or someone had helped him...

"Your friend"—he nodded towards Aurora's unconscious form—"is far too trusting. Came right to the damn gate and opened it. Didn't know if we'd have to use that option, but it worked out well."

What about the medical team? I wanted to know what happened to them, but I didn't ask. I didn't want to give him the opportunity to give me an answer that would only further throw me off.

Inhaling, I gently put Aurora down and stepped back, my steps on the stone echoing in the silence between us. I tried to search for my parents, the other dragons, or even Rachel in the crowd, but none of the faces were ones I recognized. But they recognized *me,* and the hope in their eyes had me feeling like I was going to spiral. I needed to fix this, and I had absolutely no idea how.

That was by far the most terrifying aspect of this situation. I had no idea how to fix this without bloodshed or lives lost.

Those were innocents in there: women, children, the elderly. Families who made their homes in the rogue lands. None of them wanted to be part of this war, and now they were right in the damn center of it.

"What are you planning to do? What could you possibly want?" I hissed, resisting the urge to look upwards to see if my parents had emerged to see what was going on. Holding out hope that they were hiding rather than captured.

I needed backup. I wasn't confident in taking on Linan by myself, let alone the ten guards that accompanied him—especially if they began attacking the others. *This* was why I'd needed to learn to fight.

"Well, the first depends on you," Linan said as he stepped down onto the first stair, his hands casually placed on his hips as if surveying the land around him. Despite his rather relaxed disposition, I couldn't help but notice the gashes in the arm and chest of his bloodstained clothing. I hoped one of my mates had done that to him.

The longer I looked at him, the more I realized that he was more beat up than he was letting on.

"I did plan on slaughtering them. Every last one of them. I planned on having a repeat of what happened here only eight years ago."

My fists tightened, and I focused on controlling my temper. He was goading me, trying to get me to attack him. That way he would have an excuse to react only more cruelly—to punish me by hurting those behind him. Or by capturing me.

"But..." he drew out, "I suppose I could be convinced otherwise. You asked what I wanted, but you forgot the most important question, Bexley."

"And what's that?"

"The why. *Why* am I doing all of this?"

"Power," I immediately bit out. "Your reasons don't matter though—"

"But they fucking do!" he roared, snapping in a hot second from relaxed and indifferent to red-hot rage. I stepped back, wavering in my boldness as he flashed a manic smile. "So go on, little dragon, and ask."

"What do you want and *why*?" I hissed.

At this point, without a plan, my best option was to delay until...well, obviously my mates wouldn't be coming back anytime soon. Maybe until my parents and the others made themselves known? I had no idea what I was supposed to do, but all of those people were relying on me.

"Let's start with the why," he said, taking out a pocket knife and flipping it open, then shutting it and flicking it open again and again. I knew the action was meant to be threatening, and I would have loved to say that it didn't work...but that would be a lie. "Did you know that I went to DIA with your father and his friends? That we were all there around the same time?"

When I didn't respond, he narrowed his eyes. "Well, did you?"

Why was he insistent on having me be an active part of this conversation? This was insanity. Still, I couldn't exactly refuse. "No."

"Of course not, which means you didn't know how they made my life hell. *Every. Single. Chance. They. Had.* For four years I was made to feel worthless, powerless, and they enjoyed it—they found it amusing!"

Something about that didn't sit right, but I didn't have any information to counter it.

"They always made me feel second best, so I promised myself that when I left DIA, I would never feel that way again. And for some time, we kept our lives separated. Despite all being leaders, our paths rarely crossed. I took pride that I had something they never would—dominance over the city."

"The city is ruled by all the—"

"Me," he snarled. "It's ruled by me. *Only* me. The others are just pawns. Your parents—all of the storm dragon leaders—wanted me to be a pawn as well. They wanted to consolidate power and turn all four dragon clan territories into one massive kingdom that could easily take over the city."

"That was never the plan," I whispered. Was that truly how his brain worked?

"It was. Everyone is always looking for power, and they're no different. So the 'why' is because your parents, their parents, deserve to lose everything. They deserve to feel the same way I felt when they were making my life hell—*pathetic and broken.*"

The only thing that felt pathetic was that he was willing to do all of this—sacrifice this many lives—for revenge. I had no way to know if he was telling the truth, and maybe my father and his friends had treated him horribly, but this seemed like an extreme reaction.

"That's what you want then?"

"That is what I want. Along with the territory and everyone's prized possession...*you*."

A crack of thunder and a bolt of lightning hit the ground next to me as several figures dropped from the sky. Relief immediately filled my chest as I found that Celine, Marilyn, my mom, my dad, and Rachel had arrived. But not just Rachel...

"What are you doing?" I asked my mom in a hushed whisper, panic catching in my throat. She was crouched behind me so that Clanguard couldn't see her—or the knife she held to Olivia's throat.

"I'd wondered where you'd gone. And look, you've even gained some strength back." Linan chuckled. "Good for you."

My dad stepped forward, giving me a small nod. Knowing what he wanted, I stepped to the side, revealing my mom and Olivia. Dad now served as the barrier between Clanguard and the rest of us.

Silence. Absolute silence.

"You fucking bastard." Clanguard's voice was distorted as he let out a ferocious snarl, his skin sprouting fur as if he were about to shift. *Holy crap*, talk about a reaction! I was starting to think that any part of Linan that had been 'calculating,' as his sons had regarded him, was long gone.

"It appears we've found a weak spot then," my dad said coldly, in a voice I'd never heard. "Yet somehow I find it hard to believe you care that much about your child when you had her locked up for years."

Clanguard froze, and I watched as he schooled himself, taking some deep breaths before barely getting out, "I don't give a fuck—" Olivia flinched. "But my wolf does."

"Or you do care," my father drew out. "You're something of a liar, Linan. That story you told my daughter is missing a few things, isn't it?"

"No," Linan snarled.

"Oh, I disagree. How about we discuss *why* we even noticed you in the first place? Why the women on campus were so scared of you. Why the prey shifters were treated like second-class citizens. Let's discuss how your father continuously bought your way out of trouble—until we showed up. We *did* treat you like the shit you were, because the way you treated others was inhuman."

Linan's teeth sharpened into canines. "Well, that isn't exactly wrong, is it? I mean, look what happens when that isn't the case. My own sons are fucking mated to a rabbit shifter."

"Yes, they are," Rachel voiced loudly. "And they're far better people than you." I was both surprised and beyond proud of her for speaking up for herself, especially when she hissed "jerk" under her breath.

"You had potential, Linan," Celine said. "But your own family fucked you up so bad that you treat others like they don't exist. The *only* one at fault for this is you."

"And now that you've attacked my family," my mom said, standing and keeping the knife to Olivia's throat, "I plan to do the same—but more successfully than you."

Clanguard offered a dark amused smirk. "Do it— slit her throat! The brat looks just like her mother, ungrateful bitch."

Olivia's small sob had me nearly shaking. I knew my mom wouldn't kill her, but I didn't understand what she was playing at. I didn't like the terror on the little girl's face.

I'm not sure what caused me to snap—to finally reach my limit. It may have been as simple as everything my mates and I had had to go through because of Linan, or because I was now aware of what he had others endure because of his insanity. Or maybe it was the tears on Olivia's face...but something snapped.

My dragon seeped out under my skin, and this time there was no pushing her back.

The sky cracked with thunder in a direct reflection of my anger, and I stepped forward to stand next to my dad. "You are what's wrong with this territory," I hissed, the wind increasing and my power building as I took another step forward. My dad went to grab my arm, but the lightning shimmering over the top of my skin gave him pause. "*You* make people think it's okay to treat someone worse because they aren't as big or strong. *You* are the problem, and you deserve to die because of it."

Linan moved down the steps and hit his chest with his fist. "Do it then—kill me. You absolutely do not have the will or strength to kill anyone. You are nothing, Bexley Blackforge—just a prized possession."

Lightning rocketed down from the sky, hitting the stone we stood on. Shards exploded into the air, the wind howling as I took another step towards him. The manic light in his eyes told me he wasn't going to back down, and when another surge of power hit me, I knew my mates had arrived. They were flooding me with magic, giving me the help I needed. The sky above me swirled, and an instinctual part of me knew exactly what to do.

"This ends now!" I screamed over the wind. The

guards in the doorway took cover as several things happened at once.

Clanguard darted forward and buried his half-shifted claws into my ribs, his teeth trying to slice my throat and just barely missing.

I pressed my hand against his heart, my head falling back as lightning rained down from the skies —all four lines of storm dragon power combining in me at once.

Enraged roars of my mates sounded in the sky, and my words were a whisper to the man in front of me.

"*Goodbye*, Linan Clanguard."

A wall of lightning came down from the sky, completely surrounding Linan. My skin burned, my fingers numb, but I didn't release my grasp on him until I didn't have a choice—until his skin melted away, my eyes absorbing every single moment of it.

For just a moment, everything was absolutely silent...*before my power rebounded.*

A scream left my throat as I was blasted back, a vacuum of power causing everything to shake. I was slammed into the wall of the estate perimeter, screams filling the air as my entire body radiated with pain. My gaze, though, didn't leave the corpse on the stairs. Not even as the world tried to tear itself apart in reaction to such a massive surge of power. It was like when we went through a portal times ten, storms and tornadoes threatening to lift the very earth around us.

Yet I was numb to it all. All I could hear was silence.

"Bexley!" I stared up at Jagger in surprise, realizing he'd probably been trying to get my attention for some time. I was suddenly aware of the world around me as Jagger helped me stand, but I nearly fell to the ground again when I caught sight of the estate.

Or what was left of it.

Chapter 18

Bexley Blackforge

I had thought, or maybe naively assumed, that I'd experienced magic before. After all, shifters had innate magic, which was doubly true for storm dragons. I'd experienced it before I even learned that I was one myself.

Our breed of magic was fast. Unbreakable. An unbendable, lethal force that could be deadly and explosive. *Disastrous.*

But that wasn't the only type of magic that existed in this world.

There was an older brand of magic, the type that lulled you into a state of security as it crept forward until suddenly you realized that you were surrounded, trapped within its deadly grasp. A silent killer. Or maybe in this case, *a silent savior*.

The estate had been demolished on one side,

ripped away as if it had never been there. I couldn't even see where it'd gone. It was like it'd been blown away by the force of my power, or maybe disintegrated. But where there should have been rubble and crushed bodies...there was a dome. A silvery shell of magic protectively surrounding every single individual that had taken shelter in the grand hall.

I struggled free from Jagger's grasp, falling to my knees. I stifled a sob as I took in the sight, the faces of the people whose lives I could have so easily extinguished. That I almost *had* extinguished. I could even hear the stir of people in the courtyard behind me, all of them safe.

Someone had stepped in and saved all of them—but who?

My question was answered as the dome shifted, encapsulating everyone in a bubble that floated above my head before being deposited in a clearing outside of the estate walls. Joyful voices reached my ears as the ward popped, leaving me staring at the now empty, destroyed hall. Well...with the exception of one singular individual.

Carol—Fletcher, Olivia, and Thomas's mom.

Except she was far from the broken woman I'd seen in the cells of the pack lands. This woman looked liberated. Her previously dull hair was vibrant, streaks of gold moving through it, and her bright eyes were on me with a soft smile. Her clothes were still the same, but the way she wore them made it appear that they were so much more than the rags they were.

"Cupcake, are you okay?" My mates rushed to me, helping me stand as I wavered on my feet. I could feel their intense worry over my state, but luckily my main injury—the claw marks on my ribs— were already healing.

I was so damn glad that I'd avoided his teeth.

"Is everyone okay?" I asked, my eyes on the woman walking towards me with all the patience in the world.

"Yes," Jagger assured me. "She created a ward to defend from the blast."

"Carol, right?" Breaker said loudly as the rest of our family and friends joined us. Almost immediately Olivia broke through with an excited giggle, launching herself into her mother's arms. Emotion clogged my throat as Carol buried her nose in her daughter's hair.

"Yes," she finally said and looked behind us. "But not the Carol many of you knew—not even the Carol my sons knew. Boys, please come here."

My gaze turned to find Fletcher and Thomas striding through the gates, guards blocking the entrance once more to grant us privacy.

"Mom?" Fletcher's voice was filled with shock.

"Did he finally release you?" Thomas demanded. "Where is the bastard? More than half of his forces stopped fighting all at once. We don't know what happened, but—"

"It was Bexley," Carol explained, sitting down on the stairs. "The reason that so many in the pack fought unwillingly was me." From the looks of everyone around me, I wasn't the only one who didn't understand what was going on. "I was able to enhance your father's pull as alpha—because my magic was being controlled by a singular source. A source that Bexley just extinguished."

"Please explain," my mom said. I nodded as encouragingly as I could because Carol's summary of events had created more questions than answers.

"Right." She pulled Olivia against her further and let out a tiny sigh. "Where do I even start? I suppose at the beginning."

I leaned back against Breaker's strong frame as my mates kept close, each of them touching me in some way.

"I lived my entire life hiding what I truly was— much like Rebecca." Carol motioned to the woman who stood near the back of the group, speculation and curiosity clear on her face. "I'm a half breed. I don't show many outward characteristics, but I'm both witch and wolf. I suppressed my witch's abilities most of my life, something that was fairly easy since my mother was never around. I didn't even realize I was capable of magic until I was in my teens. And when I found out, I made sure to never use it."

I completely understood what it felt like to be shocked by a part of yourself that was hidden—especially when it came with extremely powerful magic.

"When I first met Linan, I truly believed I could trust him. He said and did all the right things. He married me, made me his mate, and for a time—right until Thomas was born—everything was perfect. Until one night, we got into a fight. It came out of nowhere..." Her voice softened and her eyes narrowed on the ground nearby, no doubt at his body.

"Or *not* out of nowhere, I guess. I realize that now. He always knew, and he'd always planned to pull it out of me. Every time he got violent, my magic reacted, and eventually there was no denying the truth. I had magic, and it was something he planned to exploit.

"So instead of fighting, he made me a deal. He wouldn't hurt me or the boys as long as I used my magic to increase his influence on his people." At this her gaze turned downward, unable to meet our eyes.

"Of course it wasn't that simple. I lived in a state of fear, feeling like an axe hung over my head. But I did everything he wanted, including building those cages. Creating and giving him power-draining weapons, and even increasing his alpha power to persuade his people to fight for him.

"*I* did all of that. I may not have been the aggressor, but I will never deny my part in all of this." Her eyes welled with tears as she looked at my mom. "I am so incredibly sorry for my part in your clan being destroyed."

"No," my mom said fiercely. "I remember how scared you were of him. You didn't do any of that for *him*—you did it for the people you loved. You would've done anything to keep your children safe, and I can't blame you for that."

Tears dripped down Carol's face as she inhaled shakily. "It was around the same time he locked you up that he did the same to me, removing me completely from the boys. I knew he was worried about my influence on them, and even worse, he placed me in a cell of my own making. It slowly pulled out my magic, to the point that I couldn't even defend myself from him physically."

"So this entire time you were down there by yourself?" I asked softly.

"Me and Olivia," she said, her chin tilted up. My

eyes stung as I realized the implication of how Olivia had come about. The girl's eyes were closed as she fell asleep against her mom, finally feeling safe. "So once again he had a weapon to use against me, which is why I continued to help him. It was also why I had you take her—she was probably more valuable to him than even my sons."

"Why?" my father demanded, although his tone was filled with compassion for her situation. I had a feeling he'd known something was up, that he'd noticed something strange about how Clanguard regarded his daughter.

"Because she has magic like me," Carol whispered. "Because she could be a tool for him."

"Which is why he was so furious," Breaker concluded.

"When the other women and I were finally released, thanks to Rebecca and the team you sent, my power came back to me. I could feel Linan's anger and victory through our mate bond, and I knew he had to have found you. I was worried we wouldn't make it before he did something drastic, so I portalled us here, and right in time. Moments later and I wouldn't have been able to shield those in the great hall. But I made it, and you...*you freed me, Bexley.* You freed everyone from him."

I wiped tears from my face, letting out a shaky

breath. "I didn't know I was even able to do that..." My voice faltered. "Thank you so much for saving them."

"You're capable of that and so much more," she said softly, standing and handing her daughter off to Thomas. She came to stand in front of me, putting her hand on my cheek. "You are the future of this territory. Remember that."

Then she walked past me, and I allowed myself to fully lay eyes on Clanguard as she crouched down next to him. "This bastard could never truly love anyone—he was rotten to the core. No matter what you would've said or done, nothing would have changed it. The only thing he ever cared about was power, and that is the unfortunate truth of Linan."

"But now he's gone and we can move forward," Fletcher said.

"Yes—but we have to do something first. We have to release his magic so that the succession of alpha can happen officially. I don't want it to die with him, and considering he can't perform a ceremony right now...

"Which of you will take his place?"

My eyes widened as I backed up. This was a moment for their family. Rachel joined them as Thomas offered his brother a nod, the understanding between them clear. I swallowed as I watched Carol whisper words over the body, her hand pushing into his chest cavity and emerging with a crispy, dry piece of something. She crushed it in her hand and the breeze picked it up, spreading it around us.

The pieces lit up in flames and then smoke, circling around Fletcher and running up his skin. His body twitched as if he were resisting the urge to shift, and I couldn't help but watch in wonder as the power settled in his frame. Through my mate bond, I could feel the shift in power as our four dragons recognized Fletcher as no longer just the future alpha of his pack—but the true one.

"Never again," Carol said. "This territory will never again face another Linan."

"This territory will never be the same," Gage agreed, the sentiment resonating with the crowd.

I looked down at Linan and then at my own hands, my vision blurring as the reality of everything that had just happened began to crash down, threatening to bury me. My words were soft, but I knew my mates would hear them.

"I'm not sure if *I'll* ever be the same again."

Chapter 19

Bexley Blackforge

Two weeks later...

"Bexley, wait up!" A familiar voice had me turning as I offered Silvia a bright smile. I knew my mates were waiting for me up ahead, which is why I'd left the meeting so quickly to begin with, but I couldn't help but wait for my new friend. *One* of them, I should say...I was making a lot of new friends lately.

"Hey, what's up?" I asked, holding my folder against my chest.

The Silvershade estate was particularly busy today. Women streamed from the ballroom, having just sat through a two-hour meeting informing them of the logistics of moving forward. To say the territory was going through a change was an understate-ment, and today was one more big step towards that.

Linan had many secrets, one of which was the number of women and children he'd kept prisoner, separated from their loved ones. After the meeting we had, I was hoping everyone would feel more at ease with all of their options, whether they wanted to stay in the city or move into clan territory.

I wanted whatever they were most comfortable with. Unfortunately, with the war and the way they'd been locked up at the mercy of Clanguard's soldiers...well, I wouldn't blame them for wanting to be as far away as possible.

"I just wanted to say you did amazing in there. The girls and I were so impressed," she chirped. I gave her a big smile, happy that she thought so.

I had been nervous about presenting housing options to all the women, but the temporary solution we'd come up with while waiting on the permanent structures to be built seemed to be a big hit. I may have stolen inspiration from the structure of our dorms back home, but no one had to know.

"That's great to hear," I admitted.

"Do you want to come grab lunch with us?"

Silvia was one of the few dragons I'd met following the war. Many had returned to the clan lands as if nothing had happened, but some of the younger generation had stuck around to help. Including Silvia and her two sisters and three cousins.

Compared to many of the other shifters I'd met, dragons seemed to function a bit differently and I found I liked it. Instead of acting like many of the powerful predators in DIA, most dragons just existed in a state of nonchalance. When I asked my mates about it, they pointed out that there was no need to act aggressively when you were already at the top.

Unless you were protecting your mate from other males—they had made sure to add that part in.

"I wish I could," I said as we stepped into the foyer, my eyes darting to the door. "But we're going to look at the estate. Maybe next time?"

"Totally! Have fun!" She gave me a squeeze and darted off, giving a quick wave to my mates but otherwise saying nothing. Somehow, they even intimidated other dragons.

"Meeting go good, *mo chuisle*?" Breaker asked.

"Very," I said, waving my folder. "Although now that the excitement from the meeting is going away, I'm kind of tired," I admitted. I giggled as Gage scooped me up, Jagger grabbing the door. Maybe we could stop in the kitchen and get a peppermint coffee. There was a bit more of a chill to the air than usual, so that sounded wonderful.

"Well, get excited—they finally broke land. We're stopping there first."

"Really?!" I asked, feeling almost giddy.

"Come on." Jagger urged me into the car, and I bounced a little bit in the seat.

The day I killed Linan Clanguard, something had changed within me. I became stronger. I was still my cupcake-, sparkle-loving self...but there was more power within me, a confidence and determination that hadn't existed before. I'd killed to protect the people of this territory—and I would do it again.

I'd never considered myself a leader before, but I found myself slipping into the role a lot recently in our time away from DIA. After all, we couldn't just go back right after a war...I mean, to say there was a lot to do was an understatement.

"I can't believe they broke land already," I said as Breaker and Gage took seats up front, Jagger handing me a tablet with a map of the plans.

When the Flash clan estate was destroyed in the war, along with some villages throughout the territory, we took the opportunity to look at the four clan lands as a whole, assessing how we could improve the setup given our situation. It had of course led to a much larger discussion about power within the territory, but considering our alliance with the other shifter groups, that too had been fairly easy to figure out.

Trabea would never be the same. In some ways it would resemble the old territory, many of the older buildings staying in service, but the clans were pulling their borders farther back from the city so that the land was more evenly split. The central and northern parts of the territory would be for the dragon clans, and in the center a new estate would be built for our family. Our parents would still live in their homes, but their estates would now serve as a border for the other section of the territory.

The city, which was now all neutral territory, was expanding into villages for families who didn't want to live in the urban center but also didn't want to live under storm dragon rule. It was hopefully going to allow for a better distribution of power. We couldn't get rid of all shifter hierarchy—like alphas or clan leaders—but I didn't think it was the best idea to upset the system too much anyway. As an interim measure, we'd suggested the idea of having more councils in place, with members elected by the people.

I wasn't sure if it would go anywhere, but my hope was that it would prevent another Linan Clanguard situation from happening. Although I had no doubt that Fletcher, Rachel, Thomas, Carol, and even Olivia would ensure that. They had their own changes to the pack they were insisting upon.

"The repairs to the old Flash clan estate are going faster than anticipated," Breaker explained, "so they were able to start on ours."

"I still feel so bad about that," I murmured. It was the one thing Aurora and Dyer had asked—that it not be destroyed! And then I had destroyed it. Luckily, they hadn't been too upset, ultimately accepting that it had been the price of ridding the land of its would be dictator. They'd also agreed that since my parents were now serving in advisory positions, they could live at the estate once more and help guide it forward under their leadership.

I think Aurora and Dyer wanted a break. Aurora had been embarrassed about everything that had gone down with her 'lover,' so she'd been rather quiet on that front with the exception of apologizing a million times over. Either way, my parents were more than happy to help. Every ounce of energy they'd lost in Linan's prison was back, and they were doing everything they could to restore the damage he'd wrought.

"I'm surprised the rogue land shifters wanted to stay and not go to the city, especially since the neutral territory is so open now," Gage said. I nodded, having been surprised by that myself, but maybe they'd decided that living under my parents wouldn't be the worst thing in the world.

"Hopefully they won't mind us being within reach," I said as we sped down a long road between the Silvershades' Flicker clan lands and the Bronze-hearts' Blitz clan lands. "I know that the alliance in the city would welcome them with open arms."

Between the dragon clans and the alliance of groups within the city, the territory now had two systems of government, essentially. Two systems that would allow for the flexibility for Trabea to grow into a more modern society instead of being frozen in the past.

I mean, already the Clanguard pack had changed so much, essentially overnight when Fletcher had replaced his father. He'd opened his pack lands to non-wolves, and almost everyone else within the city had done the same. We'd always accepted non-drag-ons, but now that the other groups were following suit, the territory as a whole was wide open. Thomas, deciding to not return to DIA, had even taken it upon himself to set into motion the building of two smaller academies for shifters who decided that formal schooling wasn't for them.

I could tell Rachel had been thrilled about not going back to DIA, and more so that both of her mates were now okay with staying together instead of being split apart by their futures. It probably helped that I was nearly positive their family was going to be growing soon...I mean, I had no proof of that—*yet!* But recently she'd said a few things that seemed to be hinting toward that.

"What are you thinking about?" Jagger asked, tucking a gold strand of hair behind my ear.

"Nothing," I teased as we pulled up to a work site, the open expanse of land to all sides making me look around with excitement. I slipped out of the car, excited to see the construction crew digging to prepare a place for the foundation of our soon-to-be house...well, castle, if we were being honest.

"Can I see the tablet?" I asked Jagger, the three of them talking to one of the crew. He handed it to me, and I opened the plans and the rendering that we'd worked up.

Five stories in height and over twenty-thousand square feet, our new estate—the one I planned to hopefully marry my mates in and eventually raise our family in—would be absolutely gigantic. At the same time, I'd tried to make it as 'us' as possible. It would be luxurious but comfortable. Livable, approachable, but still have plenty of sparkles. It would have a two-floor walk-in closet, but also a garden for growing vegetables. I'd spent at least five nights straight working on it with the architect, and while there were a million things still left to pick out, I could easily see us living in it forever.

One of my favorite parts was the open balconies that would allow us space to easily shift, especially when it came time to teach our children. That had been a suggestion from my mom, and now we had three of them!

"There she is!" A cheery voice greeted me as I flashed a smile to the woman running this entire show, her hard hat and athletic outfit the complete opposite to how she normally dressed. "You excited?"

"Am I excited for you to build the storm dragon clan leaders of Trabea their dream house?" I teased Lauren. "*Understatement.* I'm really glad that Marilyn introduced us. This is going to be amazing."

"I just hope we can capture exactly what you want. Which reminds me, I meant to ask—how many kids bedrooms? I have guest suites planned, but do you have a range you want to stick between?"

My cheeks flushed, but I looked back towards my mates, deciding that I would just freakin' ask them. "Hey! Quick question—" All three of them immediately looked over, the effect of having all their attention at once still disorienting. You'd think that at this point I'd be used to it. "How many kids bedrooms?"

"Ten. Better safe than sorry," Breaker answered, then went straight back to looking at the blueprints.

"Maybe a few more...I mean, unless you don't want that, little treasure," Jagger said, my eyebrows only going higher.

"I have no idea!" I said, deciding to tease them. "That's why I asked. Figured you guys would be able to answer the hard part."

Gage appeared in front of me and examined my face with curiosity. "How many do you think is the right number?"

Nibbling my lip, I looked back at Lauren. "Let's do ten."

"I had twelve, so that's perfect—we can have an extra 'living' space on the third floor," she said, making a note on her phone. "Now, will I be able to reach you if I have questions once you go back to campus?"

"We'll all be keeping phones on us now," I said. "With everything going on, Estrid allowed the exception." I'd honestly been surprised she even wanted us back to begin with. I'd been worried her perception of us would be tainted, considering we were the reason for a literal war—but she didn't blink twice. If she had any opinions about it, she was good at masking them.

"Perfect, I'll call you soon!" Lauren said, turning

to stride towards a trailer nearby. My gaze moved across the land, and I let out a sound of contentment.

"It's going to be beautiful," I told Gage.

"It's going to be home," he agreed. "Well, once it's done. Until then…"

"School," I murmured, feeling a thrill of excitement at the concept of going back. Honestly, it wasn't something I had expected to feel.

"You guys don't mind going back, do you?" I asked him sincerely. "I know you'd probably rather be here. There are just so many things I need to learn about my own abilities—things other than being able to destroy a several hundred year old estate with pure lightning. You know?"

Gage chuckled. "Yes, I know, cupcake. Trust me, we're perfectly happy going back for the year, and if you want to continue past that—"

"Probably not," I admitted. "But maybe… Four years sounds like a lot, so let's see how we feel this summer?"

He nodded and tugged me against him, dipping his head to brush his lips against my own. "Besides," he mused, "you may be busy next summer."

With that, he walked back to the others. *What the heck did that mean?* I was completely perplexed, but I didn't bother devoting energy to the question. I knew he would explain himself eventually, and I was too happy basking in thoughts of our future here. There was a lot of hard work ahead of us, but it'd be worth it.

And until then? It was time to go back to Dark Imaginarium Academy.

Chapter 20

Gage Bronzeheart

One month later...

"Cupcake," I rumbled, catching my mate around her waist. A laugh pealed from her lips, and I smiled at the amazing sound. As she melted back into me and tilted her head back I felt taken off guard, not for the first time, by how fucking beautiful she was. The way she looked with afternoon light hitting her golden skin caused me to squeeze her tighter, feeling painfully possessive over her.

One would think that after all this time it would have faded, or at least subsided, given that I'd marked her, the others had marked her, and it was beyond clear for everyone to see that she was ours. But it hadn't, and I hoped it never would.

"Yes?" she chimed, offering me a knowing smile.

"Promise to meet me here right after class," I said pointedly.

She sighed, giving me a sassy eye roll. "Fine, fine —but only because you're being bossy," she teased. "I always meet you after class anyway."

"This time it's extra important," I said seriously, my fingers running over her waist. Despite the time of year, the chill of October infiltrating the campus, she was wearing a light silk dress with a sweater wrapped around her shoulders, along with boots. In my opinion it was far too little, but I knew clothes was a battle none of us would ever win.

"Okay, I promise," she agreed, going up on her toes and pressing a light to kiss my lips before disappearing into the classroom. Standing there for a long moment, I made my way down the hall to a bench and sat, examining the changing autumn landscape outside the window.

I could've made myself busy while she was in class—I understood that she was safe and essentially untouchable in theory—but it didn't sit right with me. Especially when I had nothing else to do. Although it was completely factual to say that no one would mess with Bexley, and it was only partially because of us.

The real reason had all to do with her. Word of what had happened and the power she'd wielded had gotten out, and the shift in the way others regarded her was immediately evident when we arrived on campus. While people weren't afraid of her—or at least most weren't—because of her softer personality, there was a natural respect and apprehension that she was now greeted with. She bulldozed through the latter completely, reaching out to make friends with both prey and predator.

Our mate was like this personal sunshine to everyone on campus, and even Diane and her crew found themselves hanging around Bexley. I wanted to be jealous about the attention she got, but I could see how she thrived off of the interactions and the sense that the community was coming together—so I shut the fuck up because her happiness was far more important than my issues.

"Hey, Gage." My head turned to see Fletcher's new beta, George, walking down the hall with his mate. Unlike Fletcher, many of the wolves who were in DIA had decided to stay, and George was one of them. The bastard was leagues better than Walker.

"Morning." I greeted him with a head nod as he approached me after his mate had slipped into the classroom.

"Bexley reached out to the wolf pack about hosting a bonfire mixer with everyone. I wanted to make sure that we were cool to do that—Fletcher's fine with it, but I wanted to clear it with everyone else."

"If she brought it up to you, assume we're good with it," I said easily. Despite my possessiveness, I had distinctly chilled out in the past month, and I could tell that it still freaked people out. George didn't appear bothered by it though.

"Awesome, I'll be in contact," he said and jogged away.

Pulling out my phone, I checked the group message with Jagger and Breaker, who were back at the dorms. Shooting off a text to let them know our ETA, I scrolled through my other messages, glad that we were able to have our phones here now. We weren't really supposed to use them except in case of emergencies, but...I think this called for an exception.

Lauren had sent us some photos of the framing of our house going up, an icon showing that Bexley had seen it. I could practically hear and easily imagine her excitement from the classroom. I couldn't wait to get her in that house. I knew that she was enjoying school, and if she wanted to continue I'd be the last to stop her, but there was also a lot of change coming to the territory. Being there to help could be essential, laying the foundation for our part as clan leaders.

I knew one thing for sure, though—we weren't waiting past this next summer to get married. I wanted our ring on her finger, which is exactly why I was so damn impatient for her to get out of this damn class. My lips pressed up, thinking about the ring we'd chosen.

"You boys brought the whole jewelry store here," my mom mused. Luckily, she hadn't gone out with Bexley and the others, somehow realizing why we were staying behind and deciding to lend her opinion. Considering how stubborn the three of us could be, it wasn't the worst idea to have an outside source who was familiar with Bexley to serve as a source of reason.

She hadn't been exaggerating, either. We had, in fact, ordered the entire store here, and the older man who owned it was more than happy to oblige. I watched as he laid out five cases of rings, all varying in size and color.

"Wanted as many options as possible," I explained.

"Just remember—big and shiny. It's Bexley." She smirked. "The girl loves shiny."

She did, but everything here fit that description. We'd even given him a four-karat minimum.

Walking up to the glass cases with Breaker and Jagger, we began to examine our options. All of them, from the white gold to the traditional gold, were beautiful, but none of them particularly stood out to me. It was missing some element of color to it, and I started to get worried we wouldn't find anything...

Reaching the last case, a huge princess cut diamond caught my attention. Around it, in a halo of stones, were a set of yellow diamonds circling it like a sun. Motioning for the others, they joined me, all of us staring at it for a long moment.

"This is the one," I told them.

"The yellow is perfect," Breaker agreed.

"And it's big enough," Jagger mused.

"Oh, let me see," my mom sang, appearing next to us. She stared at the ring in surprise, her brows shooting up. "Oh, wow."

"What do you think?" I asked.

"I think it's beautiful! And huge. I mean, that has to be—"

"Ten karats."

Shit. That was a good size.

"Perfect," Jagger said as I looked back down at the

ring, imagining it on her delicate finger. What it would look like as light shone through the diamonds onto her golden skin.

"This one. This is the one," I repeated.

To say the shop owner had been happy with our choice was an understatement, as we'd unintentionally chosen the most expensive option in the case. It probably helped that we followed it up by getting her a pair of yellow diamond earrings—which is what we'd told her we were up to when she came back early, catching the shop owner packing up. The other moms had been apologetic, but it had been the perfect cover. It had also given us reassurance that our ring was the right choice because she loved the earrings. In fact, she wore them almost daily.

I must have been trapped in thought for quite some time, because before I knew it the doors of the classroom opened and Bexley waltzed out. My eyes narrowed on some bastard behind her staring at the back of her head for a bit too long, but the minute his gaze moved to mine, he was booking it out of there. I couldn't blame the fuckers for looking at her, but I also wouldn't let it stand.

"You waited?" she teased. "I am not surprised at

all. I feel like the three of you don't even have classes anymore."

We didn't—not really—but that was because we chose not to go to them very often. I had way more important stuff to be focused on, namely my mate.

Standing up, I pulled her into me and kissed her hard. She melted against me and let out a sweet sigh, the sound enough to have me pulling back—other students were watching, and they didn't get to see this. I swept her up into my arms and strode down the hall, her laughter making me smile.

"Where are the others?" she asked, leaning her head against my chest and looking up at me as I jogged down the steps and into the fresh air.

"Back at the dorm," I said, gently setting her down. She intertwined her fingers with mine, slowing our pace down the path.

"Oh!" She turned towards me with bright eyes. "Did you see the framing?"

"It's looking good," I agreed.

"I'm hoping, fingers crossed, it's done by the end of the school year. I'd love to hold parties at it all summer." She sighed with a dreamy look. "Oh! When we eventually get married, maybe we can hold the ceremony there? We have more than enough land to make it work."

We did, and I loved that she was already in that state of mind, considering...

"I think we can arrange that," I said, lifting her left hand and brushing my lips against her soft skin. As we turned the corner, the familiar set of dorms stood out against the afternoon sky. Their pillar-like bases, leading to modern cabins up top that connected through a series of exterior bridges, had been made into a true home since returning. Bexley had gone out of her way to decorate all of them and to make the space homey, stocking us with enough food that we didn't have to leave if we didn't want to.

That wasn't the only change though.

"I would love—" Bexley's words cut off as I saw her catch sight of our surprise.

The land in the center of the dorms, surrounded by the large structure, had gone untouched for a very long time, but that had been changed now. Hanging from the bridges were lanterns that lit up the space, and a garden with hedges and a stone patio with a fire pit now filled the area. There were three comfortable benches with enough room for us to all sit, but also for her to entertain friends. I knew that she didn't always want to go to parties, but she loved having people over, so it felt like the right move.

Sprinting ahead, she nearly tackled Breaker, causing me to chuckle. Jagger jumped down from the bridge above, giving me a nod. He had what we needed.

"This is awesome!" She twirled around once Breaker set her down, Jagger using it as an opportunity to hand me the dark box. "We should have a bonfire tonight. This is the perfect space to have everyone over. Thank you guys so much."

"No problem, little treasure."

I inhaled and pushed away my nerves. After all this time, it felt ridiculous, but this woman was the center of all of our universes. I wanted to get this right.

"We can do that," I agreed. "We'll have a reason to celebrate."

"Oh?" she turned from her examination of one of the handcrafted benches, now facing the three of us. Offering the others a small nod, I decided to just fucking go for it. The minute that my knee touched the ground, the others following suit, Bexley let out a gasp. The way she held her hands over her mouth, her eyes wide, told me that we'd done our job—she'd truly had no idea that this was going to happen.

"Bexley," Breaker said, "we loved you before we even knew what love was. And even though we lost you for a period of time, our love only grew."

"You're ours," Jagger said. "Completely ours, with an entire future ahead of us."

I pulled out the box that was a deep sapphire and opened it to reveal the ring inside. "Marry us, Bexley Blackforge, and make our bond official in every single way possible."

"Yes!" she squeaked, tears filling her eyes as she nodded. "Absolutely yes. I love each of you so incredibly much, and I don't want a future if it doesn't include the four of us together."

Standing up, the three of us surrounded her. She happily put her hand out, the delicate motion making me worry that it would be too heavy—

"Oh my," she whispered. "I didn't realize how big it is! I love it." Her eyes filled with so much happiness as she kissed each of us in a swift and excited movement before looking back down at the ring. "This thing is so heavy."

"Wanted it as big as possible," Jagger said as I ran a hand up her back gently.

"I love it, and I love you guys so much...we totally have a reason to celebrate now! And a wedding to plan! Just *wait* till I tell our moms."

I had absolutely no doubt they'd be thrilled—they'd been waiting eagerly for us to pop the question for weeks now.

"Go grab your phone, we can call them." I squeezed her waist, and she jogged towards her backpack, her ring glinting as she opened the bag. Something settled in me upon seeing the piece of jewelry on her, and our group bond told me that Breaker and Jagger felt the same. I was thrilled that this start of forever was going to include two men I considered brothers. It felt right for the four of us to be together, just like Bexley had said.

The rest of our lives was going to be amazing, all because of my sweet cupcake.

Epilogue 1

Bexley Blackforge

The next summer...

"Hurry, hurry, we have to get you changed!" Rachel took my hand and pulled me towards the door of my bridal suite, my mates grumbling behind me. Waving to them, I giggled as she pulled me into the room, followed by every other woman in my life.

Seriously, the list was growing extensive. Rachel, Diane, my mom, and my mates' moms all joined us. Even Rebecca, who while moving a bit slower these days, seemed pleased to be part of it. There were others outside as well, guarding so that no one could come into the suite as I changed for the reception—all five hundred guests moving to the party tents that filled the back of our property.

That was when the true celebration would begin!

"That was beautiful!" Celine said as she unpinned my hair. "I'm so glad you did a traditional mating ceremony. I know it felt slightly old fashioned, but it was beautiful."

"I agree," my mom said. "I hadn't heard those vows spoken since the last storm dragon wedding, and in the native tongue from the Silvershade clan—that part was perfect!"

Mrs. Silvershade unzipped the back of my dress as Breaker's mom pulled out the other one. All of them were bustling around me, and all I could do was smile, captivated by my image in the mirror. My wedding gown was gold and long-sleeved, the bodice covered in jewels of black, amber, and silver, starting heavy at the top and fading to a sprinkle on the skirt. The train was several feet long, and I think my freakin' dad had almost tripped on it while walking me down the aisle.

The ceremony *had* been absolutely beautiful, held in the ballroom of our new estate. The decorations—everything from the drapery coming down from the ceilings to the handwritten programs—had been a dream. We'd limited the guest list for the ceremony, but the reception was open to anyone from the territory who wanted to make the journey. Our families had even created an entire camping area with luxury tents for people to stay in. The whole thing was...it was something else.

"I can't wait to dance," I said as the door opened and Olivia and Carol slipped in. "Olivia, you did amazing! Best flower girl ever! And Carol, the floating candles along the ceiling were gorgeous."

"Just glad we could help," she said, taking a seat.

"Alright, let's step out of this," my mom instructed, leaving me in a gold slip and heels. Rachel had already started brushing my hair from its updo, and Diane was touching up my makeup. Rebecca walked over with my reception dress, which had been handmade in the fae territory.

It was silky and uncomplicated—a bright metallic gold accented with diamonds—but gorgeous and perfect for dancing. It also complemented my bridesmaids'—Rachel and Diane's—dresses, which along with the flower girl's were bronze. My mates had worn black tuxes to round out the look, and I knew, I just knew, that it had turned out as stunning as I'd hoped it would.

I always loved a good party, but more than anything I wanted this celebration to be a true reflection of my mates and me, and so far it had been that and so much more! I still couldn't believe we'd planned it in less than a year.

"Here we go." Breaker's mom held my hand as I stepped into my second dress, the silky material sliding up my hips and the straps sliding over my shoulders. The back zipped up effortlessly, the dress fitting to me like a second skin.

"I can't decide which is my favorite," Mrs. Silvershade admitted.

"I love both," Diane agreed. "Now, where's the bottle of champagne we had in here?" Despite not being the friendliest individual at first, I found it fairly easy to be friends with Diane. In some ways, we were a lot alike. Not personality-wise, but in our sense of justice. Of course, I think her newfound loyalty to me had more than a little to do with the fact that I'd rid the world of Linan—something her mom and sisters celebrated upon meeting me.

As Diane poured champagne for the group, I moved to the vanity and grabbed the bracelet that Gage had given me on my eighteenth birthday. I hadn't been able to wear it with the other dress, but with this one? It went perfectly.

"Here we go!" Celine handed me a glass as we stood around in a circle. "Cheers!" Glasses clinked, and in a whirlwind I was whisked from the room and striding down the hallway. Around us people cheered and raised glasses, my own champagne sweet on my tongue as I looked around my home—although tonight it felt like a home for everyone.

Lauren had truly come through, not only completing the project by the start of summer, but creating a space that I knew I would be happy in forever.

"I can't believe we're finally here," I *whispered, standing in the gorgeous kitchen. A greenhouse ceiling arched over the island and continued all the way to the far side of the room. The amount of light that came through caused everything from the white diamond-like granite to the gold fixtures to sparkle.*

"Your vision come to life?" Jagger asked.

"More than I could ever imagine. I never want to leave."

"We don't have to," Breaker said, making me smile.

"You don't want to go back to school?" I teased, already knowing the answer. "That's okay—neither do I. I feel like anything I need to learn, I can do here."

"Whatever you want, cupcake." Gage opened the fridge and pulled out cupcakes, making me clap as I jumped up on the counter, immediately grabbing one.

"Let's stay here next fall. Let's focus on the territory."

It had been that simple to convince them, which told me all I needed to know about their opinions on the matter. Living here for the past two months had been amazing, and I'd already added so many finishing touches to each space—like the drawing and tea rooms—that made the gigantic property feel like home. I'd even convinced Rebecca to live with us in a separate wing of the house as a healer and counselor. Considering she'd been floating between our place and my parents' anyway, it worked out perfectly.

That had been another thing Lauren had delivered on, ensuring we had plenty of space for guests in the house's multiple wings. Those we never had trouble filling, but there were ten little bedrooms in our wing that were empty as of yet. Something I wanted to change, which I had no doubt my mates would love.

Taking another big sip of champagne, I offered an air 'cheers' to everyone we passed as we made our way across the lawn towards the central tent. I recognized so many women in the crowd, and I was so glad to see smiles on their faces. When we'd decided not to return to DIA, it was in large part because I'd been absent so much while I worked with the women who'd been imprisoned by Clanguard. Between that and helping with the new schools that Thomas had started, I realized I preferred focusing on the well-being of the territory.

It felt good to do something so much larger than simply focusing on myself and my family.

Before I could step foot in the tent, I was suddenly swept off my feet, laughter leaving me as Breaker whisked me onto the dance floor. Melting into his touch, I tilted my head back and saw the true, authentic happiness filled his expression.

"I hadn't seen this one," he said, referring to my dress. "You look stunning, *mo chuisle*."

Looking around the tent, at the hundreds of tables that stretched out onto the lawn and into three other tents, I felt a momentary sense of awe. Suspended from the ceiling were long pieces of gold fabric that moved like clouds above us, delicate lanterns swaying between them and creating beautiful patterns on the ground. The tables were covered in expensive linen, and the centerpieces were pure gold statues of dragons surrounded by white flowers. The scent of the flowers filled the air, and the upbeat music from the live band in the corner had us spinning and dancing only faster.

"I'm so glad we did this," I said, Breaker's

mismatched eyes filled with so much love that it humbled me. No matter how long we were together, I don't think I would ever fully get used to it—but I never wanted it to end.

"I'll never complain about making a public claim to you in front of hundreds of people." He leaned down and kissed me hard, bringing our dance to a halt as I let out a pleased noise.

"As long as she doesn't make those fucking nois- es," Gage grumbled, appearing behind me. "Love the dress, cupcake."

"Talking about cupcakes..." I twirled out of Breaker's arms and looked around. "Where are they?"

"I got it." Breaker kissed me hard once more before going toward the head table at the front. I couldn't see Jagger, but I knew he couldn't be far.

"There is an entire sweets table that I totally need to know the location of," I said with a teasing grin.

"It won't let you down," Gage promised, scooping me up. People around us cheered, causing me to blush. The kiss he placed on my lips took away any embarrassment, totally managing to distract me, and before I knew it he was setting me down.

My eyes widened because he was *totally* right— this could absolutely never let me down.

A table that had to be at least twenty-four feet in length was covered in three tiers of desserts, even featuring a chocolate fountain. But the thing that caught my attention? Several hundred gold cupcakes topped with glitter that sparkled like diamonds. I immediately grabbed one, not hesitating to remove the wrapper and take a huge bite.

When I looked up at Gage, I found him offering me the biggest grin. I arched a brow. "What?"

"You are so damn perfect." He kissed me again and then motioned towards the head table. "Let's go save Jagger over there while you enjoy your cupcake."

"Save him?" I asked with concern, only to realize that he'd been cornered by a group of little old ladies. I broke out in a laugh, unable to help myself. *One time.* I had brought him to a knitting group I started one time, and they were obsessed with him!

"I got this," I told Gage as I slipped through the crowd and reached them easily.

"Hey ladies!" They all turned towards me, a series of hugs and congratulations filling the air as I offered Jagger a knowing smile. After saying hello to each one of them and pointing them in the direction of the desserts, I made my move.

"I'm going to steal my husband away, if you ladies don't mind." I eased myself into Jagger's arms and he quickly pulled me away, causing another laugh to leave me.

"They're so persistent," he groaned. "I mean, they're nice…"

"It's funny," I teased. "But look—I got to save you!"

He offered me a narrowed look and tilted my chin up, pressing a hard kiss to my lips. My other mates were sitting nearby, and as Jagger pulled me to join them, the four of us in our own little bubble, I couldn't help but smile. This was perfect.

This was everything I could ever want or need.

Well…almost everything.

I planned on telling my husbands the one—or possibly way more than one—last thing I wanted on our honeymoon. Something that I swear they'd been trying to do this entire time…

To start a family.

Epilogue 2

Bexley Blackforge

Three years later...

"Ms. Bexley—"

I put a finger up to my lips in warning as the labor and delivery nurse slipped into the room, offering me an understanding smile while closing the door quietly. It wasn't that I had any intention of sleeping right now, but my mates were finally sleeping for what was probably the first time in two days. I was extremely glad I had three large reclining armchairs brought into this wing of the house, because there was absolutely no way any of them were going back to the normal wing of the house where our primary bedroom and the nursery were located. Not until we did so as a family—all eight of us.

"I just wanted to properly introduce myself," she said. "My name is Veronica. I'm part of the new team they just sent over to relieve the others."

"It's wonderful to meet you," I said sincerely. "I was actually hoping you could help me out of bed. I would love another shower, especially while everyone is sleeping."

"Of course," she whispered, helping me off the bed. I gave a big stretch, my back practically singing in relief. Veronica stayed with me as I made my way to the primary bathroom, just in case I needed help.

I'd considered giving birth at a medical center in the city, but at the end of the day I knew I would be far more comfortable at home with my mates. I was happy to see my instincts were right on this one.

"Anything else I can get you?" she asked after turning the shower on for me. Luckily, and despite what I'd just gone through, I was finding it pretty easy to do most things for myself.

"I would love some food, actually. I haven't really been hungry until an hour or so ago."

"Food, on the way," she promised, leaving me to undress and get into the shower. I'd already taken one shower today, but I'd been so panicked at the idea of being away for more than a second that it hadn't been a very good shower. This time I made sure to scrub and wash my hair and body before wrapping myself in a cozy robe. I had no doubt it would take a while to feel back to myself but honestly, I felt pretty good.

Once I was dressed in fresh, clean clothes, I made my way back to bed. The medical bed had already been removed, leaving me with a massive, double-king size bed to crawl into. Almost exactly at that moment, before I could even get comfy, Veronica returned.

"Food is on its way. I brought you a smoothie," she said happily and placed it down. "How are you feeling?"

"Really good," I said, my brows drawing together. "I'm not sure if that's normal, but I feel like I could run a mile or two right now, or even go flying."

Veronica let out a laugh. "We'll give it a little more time before we try that, but I do understand. I felt like I wanted to move my body so much right after birth. Mind you, I didn't give birth to four babies—just one."

I smiled proudly, looking at the babies who were sleeping comfortably on their dads. It was hard to imagine that it'd only been months ago that we'd learned about our growing family. Even though they'd only arrived hours ago, it felt like they'd been with us our whole lives. As if the world couldn't have existed before they did.

My mates' reactions when they'd found out had been adorable, even if they were stressed. After all, knowing that female storm dragons had litters and being confronted with the reality of it were two very different things.

"What wonderful news for a Monday! They're all so healthy," Rebecca said. I had absolutely no idea the mechanics behind being able to use magic to hear the babies' heartbeats, but she was able to both hear them and broadcast them throughout the room. She offered a hand to help me sit up, but Breaker rushed forward to support my back, the only one of the three who was still functioning somewhat normally. Gage was pacing, and Jagger was sitting with his elbows on his knees.

They weren't worried about the babies' health; it was the plural element that had them worked up. I hadn't been surprised ten minutes ago when Rebecca had announced finding four different heartbeats. I was a freakin' storm dragon! And we'd been trying so hard! I mean, seriously—like all the time.

"Four babies," Jagger said. "There are only four of us to begin with!"

Breaker made a sound of agreement, his hand smoothing up my back in a soothing pattern. Something I was appreciative of, since my body was totally sore this morning.

"How are you feeling?" Gage asked. "I can't imagine good—four babies? Four of them?"

"I'm fine," I sang happily. "Seriously. When can we tell if they're boys or girls?"

"Oh, I already know that. Would you like to know?" Rebecca asked, seemingly amused with their reactions.

I sat forward with interest, wincing slightly as I adjusted my position. "Yes please!"

"Okay, so we have—boy, boy, boy, and girl. How lovely."

"A girl," Breaker grunted. "Shit."

A giggle almost slipped out because it appeared my dad was going to be right—my mates were going to understand what it was like to be a girl dad.

"I love the little blanket swaddles you had made for them," Veronica said, pulling me from my memory and returning my attention to the real stars of the show—the four newest additions to our family.

While Jagger and Breaker each had one baby, Gage had both Ava and Leo.

The first was wrapped up in a pale lavender and the second in a deep green. While I hadn't had a chance to study their adorable little faces obsessively for hours, I had a feeling that both of them were going to have dark eyes like Breaker's one or Gage's dark green eyes.

Jagger had Adrian wrapped up in a blue swaddle and was snoring deeply. It was impressive that any of them were able to sleep and hold the babies at the same time, but I had a feeling that if I even uttered a single word for them to wake up, they'd be up instantly.

Noah, who was wrapped in a yellow swaddle in Breaker's arms, had light hair like Ava's, with a golden undertone. Whereas Adrian and Leo had dark auburn hair. I couldn't tell what color eyes Noah and Adrian would have, but I had a feeling they'd be either gold or light blue. I just thought it was amazing that despite being born at the same time, they each had such distinct differences.

Before I could tell Veronica that the swaddles had been a gift from the moms, hand-stitched by them, Ava shifted, letting out a small cry and trying to squirm. Veronica hurried over as I motioned for her to help me grab her. Gage squinted one eye open as he passed her off, then fell back asleep, adjusting Leo to lay in the center of his chest.

I pulled Ava into my arms, burying my nose against the top of her head.

"I'll leave you to it and be back soon with your food," Veronica promised. I nodded, never taking my eyes off Ava, who blinked her wide, dark eyes at me. *So beautiful.* I hadn't believed you could love someone so incredibly much from the second they were born. I mean, even at my baby shower I'd wondered what it would feel like to hold them...and then I'd promptly gone into labor three weeks early.

That had been a surprise, to say the least.

"This was beautiful," I told my mom and Celine. "Truly. Thank you so much."

"Anything for our girl," Celine said as my mom pulled me into a small side hug. It had been a long, wonderful day, and the baby shower luncheon was finally coming to a close. The party had been held at our property—I wasn't comfortable leaving our home's medical center for long periods of time at this point—but the moms and dads had handled everything. The white tents out back easily fit our hundred closest friends and family members.

It was early September, so leaves covered the

ground, and I was wearing a golden velvet dress. The only thing that could possibly ruin today was my back pain and the Braxton Hicks contractions. I was doing my best to ignore those, but they were getting progressively worse.

"Bex," Breaker said, appearing behind me. "Come take a seat, or at least take off the heels."

"I'll sit," I said, refusing to take off my glittery heels. I knew it was impractical, but I'd spent so much of my pregnancy in oversized t-shirts and feeling crappy that I fully intended to embrace fashion today. At least until I really couldn't handle it.

As Breaker led me back to our table, another contraction hit me—but this time it was different. The Braxton Hicks had been growing progressively stronger, and this one radiated through my back. It also had my stomach squeezing uncomfortably. My eyes widened when another one hit only a moment later as we finally reached our table.

Then another.

After five minutes of contractions that were only about forty-five seconds apart, I knew that I had to say something. "Hey, guys?" I called to the three of them. They looked over, the rest of the celebration continuing around us without a care in the world.

"What's up, cupcake?"

I offered a small pained smile as yet another one hit. "I think I may be going into labor. Like now."

There was a moment of silence...before they burst into action.

I'd hated the idea of stopping the celebration, but it turned out I'd been over seven centimeters dilated. My mates really hadn't expected that, but luckily it was a fairly easy labor and delivery considering the circumstances. And now we had all of them here, happily in our arms.

A knock on the door, followed by Veronica returning with the food, had the others waking up and looking around sleepily. Our sons kept sleeping, but Ava was wide awake and resting on my chest.

"We have dinner!" an older man announced before offering an apologetic smile when Veronica shushed him.

"Thank you so much," I said at a normal volume. "I have a feeling they're going to have to get used to noise anyway, so don't feel too bad."

"Let us know if you need anything else," Veronica said as they left the trays of food.

"Hey, you." I tilted my chin up as Gage came to the edge of the bed and pressed a kiss to my nose, laying Leo down next to Ava, who I placed on the bed next to me. They somehow found a way to snuggle into each other even though they were still swaddled and couldn't really move.

"You need to eat," Breaker said with a big yawn.

"And you guys need to sleep," I countered.

"We haven't done shit," Jagger grumbled. "If anyone should be sleeping, it's you. If you need to sleep for a few days straight, you're more than welcome to, treasure."

"As appealing as that sounds," I teased, "I actually feel great."

Breaker placed Noah down next to the other two before going to sort through the food, and when Jagger walked over with Adrian, all four babies were laid in a row. My eyes traced over the four of them as a swell of emotion hit my chest.

"I love you guys," I whispered.

"Love you so much," Breaker returned.

"You did amazing," Gage said, brushing his lips over the top of my head.

Jagger chuckled. "And now comes the hard part."

I smiled. "No way, they're total angels!" I had no doubt that the four of them would cause trouble, and I wouldn't lie...I couldn't wait to see what the future would bring for our family.

Epilogue 3

Jagger Silvershade

Fifteen years later...

"Hey!" My beautiful wife appeared next to me, her eyes lit with an excited light. "Do you need any help? People just started arriving."

Shit. Apparently three in the afternoon meant two forty-five. Absolutely ridiculous, if you asked me —but it didn't entirely surprise me. Everyone looked forward to Bexley's parties, especially when it was for our kids.

"I'm good," I assured her. "You said we have a larger cake for the rest of the party, right? This sheet cake will probably only be enough for the four of them." And I really didn't want them to be disappointed by it. I would've gotten our kids anything for their birthday, so when they asked me to make them a sheet cake for their fifteenth birthday—which seemed far too old since they'd only been babies yesterday—I knew I needed to get it right.

I couldn't believe they'd even remembered the one other time I made one for them two years ago—it had been on a complete whim, wanting to teach the boys how to bake. Apparently it had made quite the impression despite being simple—a basic cake with a layer of frosting on top.

"They're going to love it," Bexley assured me. "But yes, I got cupcakes also."

Thank the fates for that.

"Alright, let's do this," I muttered under my breath, carrying the cake tray and following behind her. As we crossed from the kitchen into the ballroom, I saw that the foyer and the party space were already filled with family and friends. In the nearly two decades we'd lived here, we'd held a million parties, but in some ways this was the most interesting.

Despite being remarkably wealthy and revered within our society by virtue of being storm dragons, our four oldest children were unusually down to earth. Possibly more than the four of us ever had been while growing up.

They'd insisted this year that the party be as

'normal' as possible and refused to pick any lavish themes or decor. Instead they wanted sandwiches, pizza, and baked goods. Bexley had convinced them to help her decorate with paper streamers and to create homemade birthday signs, so our wife had managed to wrangle that bit of decor out of them... but outside of that, absolutely nothing. I had a feeling what this was about—outside of them being pretty chill kids—and in a way it was amusing.

They were trying to fit in with their friends.

It wasn't something I would have normally encouraged—I thought it was good to stand out—but I also knew it was part of the process. And with them being fifteen today...well, that seemed about right for timing. As I set the cake on the catering table, I looked around the room for the kids, my eyes instead landing on Bexley.

She stood only a few feet away, talking to a few of the moms from the kids' school, her hands on her hips as she laughed. The way her head tilted back captivated me, and I paused to appreciate the beautiful sight. I had no idea how it was possible, but after nearly eighteen years of marriage, the woman still absolutely mesmerized me.

All of us had changed a lot in that time, and I thought it was for the better. Hell, leading this territory had been a massive part that had shaped us into better people. I felt like I had a far better idea of what it was like to be a prey shifter in our society, and I was now actively making an effort to ensure they were represented and protected. To ensure that no one like Linan caused a huge fucking issue again. Although Fletcher and Thomas had an iron hold on their wolves, so it wasn't something I worried about often.

What I *did* worry about was someone trying to talk to my wife. I understood completely why men kept trying to talk to her; I just wasn't fucking okay with it. As the mom group dissipated, I watched as some fucker from the kids' school, a dad of one of their friends, walked up to her. Approaching from behind, my gaze ran over my wife's jeans that clung to her hips. Her t-shirt was bejeweled with a birthday cake and matched her sneakers. It was dressed down compared to what she normally wore, but I knew she was trying to stick to the 'chill' plan the kids wanted. Our kids often said we dressed and did things that were a bit over the top, but they'd never minded it growing up, so I had a feeling it was some little assholes in their friend group who were jealous.

Still, we would figure that out in good time.

"I was telling my son that if the boys were interested, we could plan a camping trip—"

"We would love to do that," I said, causing the man to snap his gaze up. "I've been wanting to take the boys camping."

The man's eyes dimmed as I slid my hand around Bexley's waist and offered him a friendly smile. "Maybe you can take Ava to my mom's place for a girls' weekend while we're gone."

Bexley offered me a knowing smile. "That's a great idea. I'm not one for camping anyway."

"Right." The man nodded. "I'll get you that info...Jagger."

"Can't wait." I flashed a dangerous smile, and he nearly ran away. I sighed, shaking my head in disappointment. Looking down at Bexley, I found her smiling at me, an amused twinkle in her eye.

"As if I would let our wife go on a camping trip with some fucker," I scoffed, and she leaned up on her toes to kiss me.

"It was pretty ridiculous," she agreed, her gaze going distant for a moment as she looked around. "Hey, have you seen Ava?"

"No, I haven't. I assumed she was down here."

"I'm going to go check on her." She squeezed my hand and jogged into the foyer. Looking around, I spotted our three boys out on the patio, away from the party. I walked over to find Breaker watching them in amusement as they argued about something, my ears picking up the tail end of it.

"If you weren't acting like such a dumbass, this wouldn't be a problem," Leo hissed. I had no idea where he'd gotten his temper from...except that I did. Gage was completely to blame on that front. Or maybe I just saw the similarities because they had the exact same eyes. I mean, seriously, they were essentially a copy of one another, down to the hair color. It was a bit eerie, especially when Leo was this pissed.

"Dumbass?" Adrian arched a brow, his eyes—the exact same shade as mine—flashing with anger before running a hand through his dark hair. "You're the one who insulted her."

Ah. I could guess what this was about.

"Actually, you both made her cry—which is probably why you need to go apologize," Noah said, looking distressed. His gaze darted to where Fletcher was talking to his daughter. *Shit.* Breaker grunted, realizing that this was going to be far from amusing if the Clanguards got involved. We were walking on thin ice with our sons trying to spend so much time with their oldest daughter.

Noah was always the peacekeeper, similar to Breaker in a lot of ways, and not just in appearance.

So while I had no idea what had been said, I was inclined to believe an apology was necessary.

"Fuck it—fine," Leo snarled.

"Watch your mouth," I snapped. It wasn't surprising that they swore. It was something I blamed myself in large part for, but Bexley didn't love it. When I saw Fletcher offer Leo a knowing and somewhat annoyed look, I let out a long sigh.

This was going to be a complicated night.

* * *

Bexley Blackforge

"Ava?" I called out, sweeping the kids' wing of the house in search of our daughter. I shouldn't have been surprised to find her in the nursery with her two newest little brothers. Their birth a year ago had made our family ten in total.

They were still napping and wouldn't be up for probably another hour. Rebecca rocked in a chair nearby, knitting, as my mom offered me a knowing look. The two of them had offered to take twin watching duty for the day, and I appreciated it with all the commotion of the party happening. Especially now that all my attention needed to be on my daughter.

I frowned, finding Ava staring down at Charlie with a sad look on her face, her brows bent together.

"I was just visiting the boys. Are you going to bring them down when they wake up?" she asked, trying to school her features. Her dark eyes were filled with worry, though. While she definitely looked like a teenager, her wavy hair straightened and even a little makeup on her face, all I could see was my kid. I didn't even question her excuse, instead going over and wrapping my arms around her.

She leaned against me and let out a sigh.

"Come walk with me. Charlie and Marcus will be down later," I promised her. "They need a good rest because I know they won't be going to bed on time."

"We've got it," my mom assured me, her eyes filled with understanding. All four sets of grandparents had been amazing through every step of our parenting process, and while I knew they didn't always agree with how we handled things, they respected it.

As we walked out of the room and down the hall, Ava froze, refusing to make the turn towards the party. Turning towards her, I grabbed her arms and examined her face. "What's going on, honey?"

"I'm nervous. The boys are so popular; that's the

only reason anyone shows up. Even the girls are here for them."

Something I knew they couldn't care less about. In fact, there was only one girl they cared about, and Rachel and I were thrilled at the possibility—although it was more of an unspoken thing. After all, these things have to fall into place on their own.

"First of all, I don't think that's true," I said softly. "You have two amazing friends. Emily and Etro are going to arrive any minute—"

"Ava!" Etro's voice echoed loudly through the hallway perpendicular to ours. It was unsurprising that he'd come to find her. In fact, I could almost bet that he'd been able to somehow sense her unease. Ever since they'd been little, the two of them had an odd sense of each other's emotions. Once again, I could have guessed what it meant, especially since he was a fire-based dragon, but I would just wait and see.

"Over here." She immediately lightened up, the tension in her draining until she was almost back to normal. I could tell it wasn't forced, either—she was simply that comforted by his presence.

As he turned the corner, I nearly shook my head. I'd always assumed that my boys would be taller than most, a lot like my mates, but it did surprise me when it came to other kids their age. Specifically, Etro. He was a year older than Ava, having just turned sixteen, and somehow was over 6'3" already. Lanky and a bit awkward, to be sure, but as tall—if not taller—than my boys.

It also hadn't surprised me when the four of them had become friends, which is how he'd met Ava in the first place—on the playground, helping her up after she'd fallen off her bike.

"What's wrong?" he asked, immediately concerned. "Why aren't you down at the party?"

"I'm kind of nervous," she admitted, not embarrassed about it in the least. Ava was a lot quieter than her brothers, and not in a bad way—they just often overpowered conversations, so when she did say something, I always made sure to listen. She was also a bit of a bookworm, always finding her way into the library to read and study. It was something I'd always encouraged, but I could tell she was starting to think it was a bad quality because she wasn't as outgoing as her brothers.

I hoped we could change her mind about that.

"Don't be, your brothers have already messed up," he said. "All the attention is on them."

"What did they do? Did they hurt Mia's feelings?"

"Yep." He sighed. "Emily is over there helping, but you know how that can be." Emily was his sister and one of Ava's best friends. She was also best friends with Mia, who was Rachel's oldest daughter, and the girl that my sons had apparently 'messed up' with.

"Hi, Mrs. Blackforge," Etro suddenly said, looking embarrassed. "Sorry I didn't say hi right away."

"You're good," I promised him. "Let's just go down to the party."

Trailing behind them, I watched as my daughter's mood took a one-eighty, and I couldn't help but smile at what their friendship brought her. As we entered the foyer and walked towards the ballroom, I felt a sense of fulfillment at everyone under our roof for their birthday. Following Ava and Etro toward the patio, I slid in right next to Gage and Breaker, seeing that Jagger was over near Mia, talking to Fletcher.

"Any chance this will be resolved soon?" I asked, my brow dipping. "Did they really mess up that bad? I know they don't mean to, but if they're being jerks—"

"No." Gage sighed. "It wasn't like that. Leo got jealous of Mia talking to someone, and then Adrian asked her why she would pick such a shit friend...and then it escalated from there."

Well, considering Noah had an arm around her

shoulder right now, trying to comfort her, it didn't look like the situation was completely unmanageable. Mia was a bit of a sensitive soul, but in the best way possible. When Jagger walked over a few minutes later, I reached out and offered my hand as he pulled me against him..

"Do you remember when we were this messy?" Jagger grunted, pressing his lips to my forehead.

I offered them all a winning smile, turning in his arms to face the other two. "You know what, I actually *do* remember."

Breaker chuckled as Gage shook his head at my joke, kissing the top of my head. As the others started walking towards us, I offered my four oldest an encouraging look. "Alright, everyone good?"

"Yeah," Leo grunted. "We're good."

As they all made their way past, I offered Mia a soft smile and she offered one back, reminding me so much of my best friend. Which reminded me...

"What did I miss?" Rachel asked, her newest bunny shifter on her hip. The toddler played with her mom's pink hair before letting out an adorable yawn.

"Hello, Odelia." I poked her little nose gently, making her giggle. "You know how the boys are. Just a bit too blunt for their own good."

"And you know how Mia can be," she added

knowingly. "Well, better to get the fights done now before they realize they're mates."

I broke out into laughter because yeah...that was pretty obvious to everyone.

Except to them. They would figure it out, though.

Just like my mates and I had.

Flash concludes The Storm Dragons' Mate series. While writing this series I fell in love with Bexley and her mates, so I hope you loved their *happily ever after*! As always, thank you so much for your support. Happy reading!

Series Within DIA Universe

Monarchs of Hell (Completed Series) by R.L. Caulder and M. Sinclair

    Insurrection: mybook.to/Monarchs1

    Imbalance: mybook.to/Monarchs2

    Inheritance: mybook.to/Monarchs3

Dark Imaginarium Academy Series

    Phases of the Moon by M. Sinclair

    The Creatures We Crave by R.L. Caulder

    The Storm Dragons' Mate by M. Sinclair

    Blood Oath by R.L. Caulder

Love Bexley?! Meet Maya!

Description

I have spent my entire life in the basement of my father's church. My sadistic mother and god-fearing father believe I have the devil inside of me because I heal after their abuse. I'd accepted long ago I would die in the very place I'd been born without ever feeling the sun on my skin. Then one day, my mother took me from my father's religious cult in the wake of his death. Nearly a week later, and after countless hours with her boyfriend Jed's creepy remarks, I find myself in Washington State. I had only ever interacted with my parents and now Jed, so you can imagine my surprise when I ran smack dab into possibly the most handsome man in the world. He's not alone though, there are intriguing and handsome men popping up everywhere in my life.

Except I shouldn't be focusing on that. I should be preparing for my mother's cruel hits. Preparing to run the minute I turn 18. Preparing to hide from Jed's leering comments and uncomfortable stares. One interaction with this man and I feel like my entire life has been altered.

Five days until I turn 18. *Five days* until my mother realizes what happens when you keep a bird cooped up for too long, only to open its cage. *Five days* until I am out of here.

My problem? Everything inside of me tells me that those intriguing men are mine... and they seem to think the same.

This is a slow/medium burn fantasy RH that features a naive but strong MFC with a troubled past and a secret about what she really is. Come meet Maya and her protective and possessive dragon shifters! This book will be part of the **Reborn** series.

Warnings: Please be advised that the book contains darker themes such as child abuse, PTSD, swearing, and violence. Additionally, sexual themes are suitable for mature audiences +18. This book will end on a slight cliffhanger.

* * *

Prologue

Marco

We pulled into town and the faint scent of the shoreline assaulted my nose through the open window of the car. It brought a small smile to my face. *Home.* Not the home I'd been born in. Not the family I'd been born into. No, this was my home. A home that my flight and I had chosen for ourselves. Washington State. We lived in a small town that wasn't known for anything except the massive light-house it featured. It was why we loved it. After everything we've been through, we craved the peace and serenity it had to offer.

"Want anything from inside?" I asked Atlas. He grunted with a shake of his head before he closed his eyes once more. Our drive from Los Angeles had exhausted both of us and the reason for being there had left us both ready to sleep for the next week. I parked my BMW at the pump before standing up to go inside. My dress pants were wrinkled and my hair laid in a million different directions. What I needed right now? To get home and take a long fucking shower before passing out.

Did I need to emphasize anymore how much I needed sleep right now?

Instinctually, I categorized the one other car, a

black rusted-out Ford, parked in front of the gas station shop. There was a larger woman inside in the passenger seat, but the windows were tinted, so I couldn't get a good look at her. Something about the car made me feel off. I put it from my thoughts as I entered the shop and crossed the broken tiled floor to pay for my tank of gas. Outside, the gloomy sky thundered as it began to spit out heavy rain.

I turned toward the bathroom and made my way down the aisle, only to be run over by a young boy. I grunted as the small frame collided with my chest and swayed on their feet. A hiss of pain came from the figure as I steadied them with a solid grip on their small arms.

"Sorry," the soft voice murmured quietly.

"No problem..." I stopped talking as my eyes widened. My hands tightened on the small frame as *her* hood came down. The person I'd thought a boy was, in fact, a young woman. My dragon hissed in recognition as a pair of soft brown eyes, speckled with gold, stared back at me.

I immediately picked up the scent of sea salt, ashes, and roses on her golden skin. It was obvious she wasn't human, but I couldn't for the life of me recognize her scent. Instead, I categorized every element of her soft, wavy chocolate hair that shimmered with gold streaks and fell to her waist once released from her hood. She had the tiniest button nose and thick dark lashes that fluttered nervously. It was possible that she was the most feminine woman I'd ever met. She was just so damn beautiful. Like a rose or something equally as beautiful.

Then I noticed the way her soft pink mouth twisted in pain. I loosened my tightening grip on her thin shoulders. Why was she so thin? Did she need food? We could get her food. Also, a jacket. This wasn't heavy enough for how cold it was.

Fuck. My dragon was in a protective overdrive. This was bad.

"I need to go," she muttered, her voice raspy.

Was she sick? Why was no one taking care of her? If she wanted, I could take care of her. As in, she could come home with me to our flight house. Now. She would have literally anything she ever wanted. *And* I was going to lose my mind if I didn't learn this woman's name.

"Maya," a voice growled from behind her, "leave this man alone."

The woman shrunk down into herself, like a wilted flower. Her eyes took on a dull shine as a massive man, nearly matching Atlas' 6'5" height, appeared over her shoulder. He looked like a mean son of a bitch, but completely human. Those black eyes took note of my hands on Maya and a yellow-toothed sneer took over his face.

"Get in line buddy, she's a fucking tease," he chuckled, grabbing her hood in a taunting manner before pulling her toward the door.

I yanked her back to me, not caring about the obvious show of supernatural strength, wanting her against my chest. Safe there. My instincts were begging me to hide this woman from him. Maya. What a beautiful name. A worried whimper came from her throat as the man in front of us grew red in the face.

"It's fine," she mumbled softly before stepping out from behind my back.

Why was she resigned to his obvious disrespect? I didn't think this man was her father, but who was he then? Was this the person put in charge of watching her? I slipped a thin business card into her jogger pockets and realized she was even thinner than I'd assumed. God. I wanted to help her, but the look in her eyes told me it wasn't the time. No matter. I had her scent. I would find her.

"Come on little bitch, back to the car," the man snarled before herding her out the door. She looked back only once before offering me a barely-there smile. I felt my heart thump with deep low strums. My dragon roared aggressively in my head. He didn't care what she wanted or what the man wanted. He wanted her back here.

I didn't disagree.

"Who the hell was that?" Atlas' low baritone voice asked from the door. His eyes were filled with gold and the realization she had affected both of us had my mind working overtime.

The black truck squealed out of the gas station. I could see her faint outline from the back as the man in the front opened his mouth in what I assumed were screams. It didn't matter though, I would find her. I would help her.

"That is," I sighed as the distance grew and my heart squeezed uncomfortably, "our mate."

Read the **completed series** today:

https://geni.us/Reborn 1

M. Sinclair

M. Sinclair is a USA Today Best-Selling Author who can be found writing or thinking about her characters and plots nearly every moment of the day. With over 65 published works since her debut in 2019, her work spans from paranormal to contemporary romance rooted in extensive world-building and deep character development. M. Sinclair believes there is enough room for all types of heroines in this world, and that being saved is just as important as saving others.

Just remember to love cats... that's not negotiable.

Published Works

M. Sinclair has crafted different universes with unique plotlines, character cameos, and shared universe events. As a reader, this means that you may see your favorite character or characters... appear in multiple books besides their own storyline.

Universe 1

Established in 2019

VENGEANCE

Book 1 - Savages

Book 2 - Lunatics

Book 3 - Monsters

Book 4 - Psychos

Complete Series

Vengeance : The Complete Series

THE RED MASQUES

Book 1 - Raven Blood

Book 2 - Ashes & Bones

Book 3 - Shadow Glass

Book 4 - Fire & Smoke

Book 5 - Dark King

Complete Series

A Raven Masques Novel - Birth of a Raven

TEARS OF THE SIREN

Book 1 - Horror of Your Heart

Book 2 - Broken House

Book 3 - Neon Drops

Book 4 - Snapped Strings

Book 5 - Fractured Souls

Book 6 - Shattered Galaxies (TBA)

DESCENDANT

Book 1 - Descendant of Chaos

Book 2 - Descendant of Blood

Book 3 - Descendant of Sin

Book 4 - Descendant of Glory

Book 5 - Descendant of Pain

Book 6 - Descendant of Victory (TBA)

REBORN

Book 1 - Reborn In Flames

Book 2 - Soaring In Flames

Book 3 - Realm Of Flames

Book 4 - Dying in Flames

Book 5 - Ruling in Flames

Complete Series

THE WRONGED

Book 1 - Wicked Blaze Correctional

Book 2 - Evading Wicked Blaze

Book 3 - Defeating Wicked Blaze

Complete Series

The Wronged: Completed Series

LOST IN FAE

Book 1 - Finding Fae

Book 2 - Exploring Fae

Book 3 - Freeing Fae

Book 4 - Loving Fae (TBA)

* * *

Universe 2

Established in 2020

AMONG SHADOWS

Book 1 - Court of Betrayal

Book 2 - Court of Deception (TBA)

* * *

Paranormal & Fantasy Series

THESE SERIES ARE NOT CURRENTLY AFFILIATED WITH A SPECIFIC M. SINCLAIR UNIVERSE.

HUNTER'S MOON RITUAL

Book 1 - Howling Love (TBA)

Book 2 - TBA

Book 3 - TBA

PHASES OF THE MOON

Book 1 - Lunar Witch

Book 2 - Blood Witch

Book 3 - Shadow Witch

Book 4 - Unblessed Witch (TBA)

THE STORM DRAGONS' MATE

Book 1 - Blitz

Book 2 - Flicker

Book 3 - Surge

Book 4 - Flash

Complete Series

THE DEAD AND THE NOT SO DEAD

Book 1 - Queen of the Dead

Book 2 - Team Time with the Dead

Book 3 - Dying for the Dead

Complete Series

The Dead and the Not So Dead: Completed Series

SILVER FALLS UNIVERSITY

Book 1 - Lost

Book 2 - Forgotten

Book 3 - Discovered

Book 4 - Pursued

Book 5 - Found

Complete Series

I.S.S.

Book 1 - Soothing Nightmares

Book 2 - Defending Nightmares

Book 3 - Defeating Nightmares

Book 4 - Loving Nightmares

Universe Standalone Novel - Mating Monsters

Complete Series

* * *

Contemporary Universe

Established in 2021

THE SHADOWS OF WILDBERRY LANE

Book 1 - Perfection of Suffering

Book 2 - Execution of Anguish

Book 3 - Carnage of Misery

Complete Series

Complete Collection: The Shadows of Wildberry Lane

THEIR POSSESSION

Book 1 - Sheltered

Book 2 - Searched (TBA)

* * *

Standalone Novels

Peridot (Jewels Cafe Series)

Time for Sensibility (Women of Time)

Of Claws & Chaos (Forgotten Kingdoms)

WILLOWDALE VILLAGE COLLECTION

A collection of standalone novels about the women of Willowdale Village.

Voiceless

SEASONS OF THE HUNTRESS

Winter Huntress

* * *

Collaborations

MONARCHS OF HELL

(*M. SINCLAIR & R.L. CAULDER*)

BOOK 1 - INSURRECTION

BOOK 2 - IMBALANCE

BOOK 3 - INHERITANCE

Complete Series

FALLEN DESTINY

(*M. SINCLAIR & R.L. CAULDER*)

BOOK 1 - WINGS OF STARS

BOOK 2 - WINGS OF PAIN

BOOK 3 - TBA

THE VAMPYRES' SOURCE

(*M. SINCLAIR & R.L. CAULDER*)